SACRAMENTO PUBLIC LIBRARY
828 "I" STREET
SACRAMENTO, CA 95814
8/2024

SO-EJI-567

EVERYTHING

WE

NEVER

HAD

EVERYTHING

WE

NEVER

HAD

RANDY
RIBAY

Kokila

ALSO BY RANDY RIBAY

An Infinite Number of Parallel Universes

After the Shot Drops

Patron Saints of Nothing

Avatar, The Last Airbender: The Reckoning of Roku
(Chronicles of the Avatar, Book 5)

KOKILA

An imprint of Penguin Random House LLC

1745 Broadway, New York, New York 10019

First published in the United States of America by Kokila, an imprint of Penguin Random House LLC, 2024

Copyright © 2024 by Randy Ribay

Grateful acknowledgment is made for permission to reprint an excerpt from "Resolution Flaying Filipinos Drawn by Judge D. W. Rohrbach" published in *The Evening Pajaronian*, January 10, 1930. Used with permission.

Penguin supports copyright. Copyright fuels creativity, encourages diverse voices, promotes free speech, and creates a vibrant culture. Thank you for buying an authorized edition of this book and for complying with copyright laws by not reproducing, scanning, or distributing any part of it in any form without permission. You are supporting writers and allowing Penguin to continue to publish books for every reader.

Kokila & colophon are registered trademarks of Penguin Random House LLC.

The Penguin colophon is a registered trademark of Penguin Books Limited.

Visit us online at PenguinRandomHouse.com.

Library of Congress Cataloging-in-Publication Data

Names: Ribay, Randy, author.

Title: Everything we never had / Randy Ribay.

Description: New York: Kokila, 2024. | Includes bibliographical references. | Audience: Ages 12+ | Audience: Grades 7–9. | Summary: "Set in the 1930s to today, four generations of Filipino American boys grapple with identity, masculinity, and father-son relationships"—Provided by publisher.

Identifiers: LCCN 2024010379 (print) | LCCN 2024010380 (ebook) | ISBN 9780593461419 (hardcover) | ISBN 9780593461433 (epub) | ISBN 9780593866733 | ISBN 9780593866740

Subjects: CYAC: Family life—Fiction. | Fathers and sons—Fiction. | Filipino American—Fiction. | LCGFT: Novels.

Classification: LCC PZ7.1.R5 Ev 2024 (print) | LCC PZ7.1.R5 (ebook) | DDC [Fic]—dc23

LC record available at https://lccn.loc.gov/2024010379

LC ebook record available at https://lccn.loc.gov/2024010380

ISBN 9780593461419 (HARDCOVER)

ISBN 9780593857168 (INTERNATIONAL EDITION)

1st Printing

Printed in the United States of America

LSCC

This book was edited by Namrata Tripathi, copyedited by Kaitlyn San Miguel, proofread by Jacqueline Hornberger, and designed by Jasmin Rubero. The production was supervised by Tabitha Dulla, Nicole Kiser, Ariela Rudy Zaltzman, and Lisa Schwartz.

Text set in Albertina MT Pro

This is a work of fiction. All incidents and dialogue, and all characters with the exception of some well-known historical figures, are products of the author's imagination and are not to be construed as real. Where real-life historical persons appear, the situations, incidents, and dialogues concerning those persons are entirely fictional and are not intended to depict actual events or to change the entirely fictional nature of the work. In all other respects, any resemblance to persons living or dead is entirely coincidental.

The publisher does not have any control over and does not assume any responsibility for author or third-party websites or their content.

For my son
and my father
and me

With the arrival of every boatload of Filipinos, a boatload of American men and women are thrown out of the labor market to lives of crime, indolence, and poverty because, for a wage that a white man cannot exist on, the Filipinos will take the job and, through the clannish, low-standard mode of housing and feeding, practiced among them, will soon be clothed, and strutting about like a peacock and endeavoring to attract the eyes of the young American and Mexican girls. . . . We do not advocate violence, but we do feel that the United States should give the Filipinos their liberty and then send those unwelcome inhabitants from our shores that the white people who have inherited this country for themselves and their offspring might live.

—Judge D. W. Rohrbach, Justice of the Peace, 1930

We are the living dream of the dead. We are the living spirit of the free.

—Carlos Bulosan, from *America Is in the Heart*, 1943

MAGHABOL

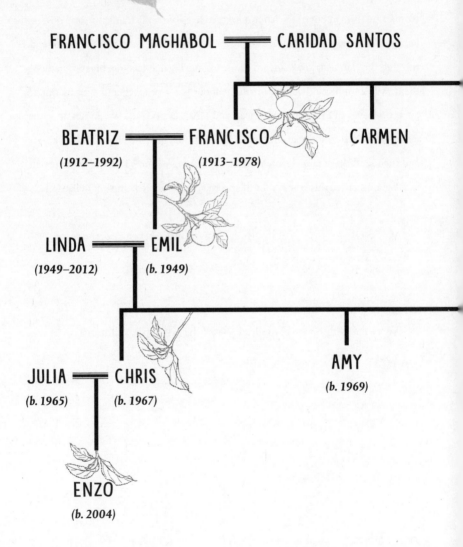

FRANCISCO MAGHABOL ══ CARIDAD SANTOS

BEATRIZ ══ FRANCISCO   CARMEN
(1912–1992)   *(1913–1978)*

LINDA ══ EMIL
(1949–2012)   *(b. 1949)*

JULIA ══ CHRIS   AMY
(b. 1965)   *(b. 1967)*   *(b. 1969)*

ENZO
(b. 2004)

FAMILY TREE
(INCOMPLETE)

```
┌──────────────┬──────────────┬──────────────┐
│              │              │              │

JUAN LUIS         JOSÉ          XAVIER
```

```
┌──────────────┐
│              │

JENNY
(b. 1973)
```

FRANCISCO

October 1929
Watsonville, CA

THE FOG

The fog cloaks the orchard in the cold pre-dawn darkness. It holds the Pajaro Valley close as a secret, reducing everything to a suggestion of itself. Muted shapes emerging, dissolving.

The hills on the horizon. The shallow-rooted apple trees growing in straight rows. The silent brown men, young and old, shaking off dreams as they drift, unmoored, through the haze on their way to begin the day's work.

Francisco Maghabol is among them, shouldering a heavy wooden ladder, with an empty burlap sack slung across his chest. Faded hat, worn gloves, threadbare clothes. Sixteen years old now, fifteen when he stepped into the belly of the boat that carried him from Manila to Japan to Hawai'i to California. Across the sea to where the streets were strewn with gold—at least that's what the missionaries and the teachers and the ticketing agents and the leaflets and the Hawai'ianos had said. And it had seemed to be true from the faded and folded pictures sent home and passed around the villages from the returning pensionados flush with cash and American goods.

It turned out there was no gold. At least not for him or his kailian, not here, not by the time they'd arrived. Only a contract they had to sign before they could leave the steamship's hold. Only old-timers asking to borrow money. Only blisters and calluses, sore muscles and bad backs, skin that never stopped itching from the fine dust of the fields. Only *Go back to where you came from!* and a dollar a day, not enough to eat—despite picking the peas and beans and grapes and strawberries and cherries and apples and oranges and lettuce and asparagus and artichokes and garlic that fed this ever-hungry nation. His nanang would say, *Sasáor banbannóg no sabali ti aglamlámot*—useless labor when eaten by others.

As Francisco and the other field laborers reach the apple orchard, they hoist their ladders off their shoulders and position them against the trees. Silent and sullen, the men ascend into the branches. But Francisco hesitates. On mornings like this—when he is near the world but not in it, near the others but not with them, near himself but not quite; when the fog has seeped through his skin and settled into his bones and he no longer knows where it ends and his breath begins, having already filled his lungs with too much mist—he wonders if he should have listened to his nanang.

Maybe leaving wasn't the only way.

He had felt like such a man then. The eldest son venturing into the unknown to do what he must to take care of his nanang and sister and brothers after his tatang lost their land and left them for the woman with the mole on her right earlobe. The plan had seemed simple enough from a distance: work in America for three—maybe four—years, make enough money to pay his younger siblings' school fees and to buy back his family's land, then return to work it.

But now?

He isn't so sure.

Not a man. No longer a boy. Maybe more so a ghost, since duty dissolves as it absolves.

Still standing at the base of his ladder, Francisco watches Lorenzo

Tolentino in the next row over shake a pebble out of his glove. The same ship—the *President Jackson*—had carried them across the sea. They found each other in the crowded, swaying dimness of the third-class hold after hearing home in each other's voices and discovering they hailed from neighboring villages in Ilocos Sur. Since then, they'd stuck together, following the planting, then harvesting seasons along the coast for one full cycle. Other Ilokanos would join them from time to time to form small temporary crews so it would be easier to find work. But they'd always peel away, one by one, until only Francisco and Lorenzo remained.

Thoughtful, quiet Lorenzo. Nineteen to Francisco's sixteen. Medium brown skin, wide nose, and a smile as smooth as a shoreline. A high school graduate from an educated family, toiling for tuition so he could attend college in America and become a lawyer.

Lorenzo slips his glove back on and glances at Francisco. "Something wrong, little brother?" he asks in Ilokano.

"You ever regret coming here, Manong?" Francisco says.

Or, at least, he wants to.

The question has begun to germinate in his soul. He feels like if he doesn't ask someone soon, he might burn off into the atmosphere with the fog when the late-morning autumn sun splits the clouds. He needs to know he is not alone.

Because as much as he and Lorenzo have been through together, they've never discussed regret or loneliness or anything else of consequence. They've never named what they've most deeply felt because naming a thing means you must confront it. It means lighting a candle to illuminate what's lurking in the shadows. Sometimes the only way to survive is to not know.

Francisco wipes the condensation from the rungs of his ladder as he wonders how to say what he feels. Sometimes trying to do so is like fishing with a net badly in need of repair.

In the end, he takes off his hat and smooths his hair back. "I'm okay."

Lorenzo nods and climbs up his ladder. Francisco puts his hat back on and does the same a moment later. Parallel, wordless, and with practiced hands, they begin plucking the ripe red apples from the branches. They work quickly but carefully since the fruit's skin is slick with dew and the early-morning watering.

Can this ever be enough: picking fruit in thick fog, filling sacks to fill crates to fill trucks to fill the stomachs of those who will never spend their days in fields?

Could this ever be enough to quiet the regret, to justify an ocean crossing, to anchor him to the earth?

Francisco does not yet know.

ENZO

December 2019–February 2020
Philadelphia, PA

UTANG NA LOOB

Enzo gazes at the two pounds of lumpia mixture in the middle of the table as he takes his seat. He breathes in the familiar scent of raw ground pork, soy sauce, patis, garlic, and minced vegetables wafting from the large bowl, his freshly washed hands already aching in anticipation of the hundred or so lumpia he'll roll over the next couple of hours.

His mom, Julia, sits to his right. His dad, Chris, to his left. In front of each member of the family: a sheet of tinfoil, a spoon, a finger bowl of water, and a square stack of paper-thin egg roll wrappers, thawed overnight in the refrigerator. The house is dark except for the dining room light. Old-school R & B plays softly from the Bluetooth speaker in the kitchen. Outside, Christmas lights shimmer, and a damp snow falls with flakes that melt as soon as they touch the concrete.

Enzo cracks his knuckles and rolls up his sleeves. "Death by lumpia," he mumbles.

"¡Qué gracioso! Siempre con el mismo chiste," Julia says. "You need some new material."

"That's how we roll," Chris says.

"Like father, like son." Julia shakes her head. "Unfortunately."

Chris smirks as he lays out wrappers across his sheet of tinfoil. "I'm sure Enzo had a very difficult day watching TV and playing video games. He probably needs to rest."

Enzo looks up, skeptical. "So I don't have to help?"

"Of course you don't, anak," Chris says, then begins to plop a spoonful of filling just below the center of each wrapper. As Enzo moves to leave, Chris adds, "But remember: no help, no eat."

Enzo sighs, gets to work.

Spoon. Shape. Tuck. Fold. Roll. Dab. Roll. Stack.

Spoon. Shape. Tuck. Fold. Roll. Dab. Roll. Stack.

Spoon. Shape. Tuck. Fold. Roll. Dab. Roll. Stack.

"Kyle told me they sell these pre-made in the frozen section at the Asian grocery store," Enzo says after some time.

Chris raises his eyebrow. "Have you tasted them?"

"No."

"You're welcome."

Julia laughs as she stacks one more on the plate with the others she's already finished.

"Don't encourage him, Mom," Enzo says.

"Dapat kang magpasalamat," Chris says in Tagalog. "I had to teach myself because—"

"Because Lolo Emil is an assimilationist."

"Ah, so I've told you before?"

"Once or twice."

"As they say, 'Ang hindi marunong lumingon sa pinanggalingan ay hindi makakarating sa paroroonan.' Therefore it's our responsibility to carry on the cultural practices of our Philippine ancestors."

"Y también nuestras tradiciones boricuas," Julia adds. "Which is why we're making coquito tomorrow."

"I get it," Enzo says, having grown up steeped in—and, at times, overwhelmed by—the languages and foods and traditions and histories of both sides of his family. "It's just kind of boring doing the same thing a thousand times."

"Consider it family bonding."

"I like to think of it as meditative," Julia says. "Inhale"—she inhales deeply as she shapes the filling, then tucks the corners of the wrapper—"and exhale." She exhales deeply as she rolls.

The three continue to work, falling into a familiar rhythm. Chris moves slowly and carefully, each of his lumpia tightly rolled with the exact amount of filling. Julia rolls three times as fast, the quality inconsistent. And then there is Enzo with his, lumpy and loose, the top folds sure to unfurl like little capes when they're frying in the hot oil later.

As they roll, they talk. About their days. About what Enzo plans to do with the rest of his winter break and if he wants to play football next year after spending most of his sophomore season—which ended just a few weeks ago—on the sidelines. About the research Julia's star PhD candidate advisee is doing on social justice mathematics. About the Model UN club's trip to Germany in the summer that Chris is organizing as the club's advisor.

The music plays. The snow falls and melts. The pyramid-shaped stack of rolls rises as the mixture in the bowl disappears. After the three finish and take turns washing their hands, Chris carries the dishes to the sink, Julia wipes down the table, and Enzo Saran Wraps the plates with the lumpia and slides them into the fridge. Chris will fry them right before they leave for the Philly Fil-Am Association's New Year's party so they're as fresh as possible.

Julia says good night, hugs Enzo and Chris, then retreats upstairs, leaving them with the dishes.

"Wash or dry?" Chris asks.

"Dry," Enzo says.

Chris tosses Enzo a clean dish towel and takes his place at the sink. He turns on the faucet and fidgets with the handle to adjust the temperature. "There's actually something I want to speak to you about."

"It's a trap!" Enzo says, using his best Admiral Ackbar impression. A joke to distract himself from the tightness that pinches his chest at his dad's suddenly somber tone. Will this be about his first-semester grade in history? Did his mom find a new position at a different university? Has Titi Camila's cancer returned?

Chris squirts dish soap onto the sponge and starts washing the first dish. "What would you think about your lolo Emil moving in with us?"

Surprise replaces Enzo's concern. "Your dad?"

Chris nods and hands Enzo a clean plate.

Enzo takes it. Towels it off. Places it in the drying rack. "But you hate him."

"He's my father, Enzo. I don't hate him."

"You don't like him."

Chris doesn't deny it.

None of them, in fact, like Lolo Emil. And the feeling is mutual. He is the kind of person who chooses to mispronounce Julia's name. Who constantly reminds Chris he's a disappointment for becoming a middle school teacher instead of an engineer. Who scoffs at Enzo's anxiety diagnosis, insisting he has nothing to complain about. Who refuses to visit his two daughters who live in California because it's California.

After Enzo's grandma Linda passed away several years ago, Lolo Emil moved into a retirement community on the Main Line and announced that he would let them know when he wished to see them. It turned out he did not wish to see them much.

"Why?" Enzo asks.

His dad hesitates in the way he does when he's afraid of triggering Enzo's anxiety. "Remember my friend Dr. Young?" he finally says after a few moments.

Enzo nods, but it's a weird question. Dr. Young is one of his dad's oldest friends and Enzo's ninang.

He passes Enzo a bowl to dry. "She said she heard about this new virus. In China. It's probably nothing. But she knows my father's living in a retirement community, so she suggested we consider moving him out. Just to be safe."

"She's afraid it's going to spread? All the way from China?"

"It probably won't."

"But it might?"

"It probably won't," Chris repeats.

Enzo remembers the bowl and dries it, noticing his heart rate has increased. "And this virus—it's pretty bad?"

Chris shrugs. "There are a lot of unknowns, but Dr. Young said it might be really contagious, which is not great when people live close together, like they do in nursing homes. That's worst-case scenario, though, Enzo. Every other year it seems like there's some new disease everyone's afraid is going to ravage the world. You hear about it for a few weeks, and then what? It's gone. Maybe we've all been watching too many postapocalyptic movies."

"I don't think the people affected by those diseases would agree with that idea," Enzo says. "But has Dr. Young told you to do anything like this before?"

Chris is quiet for a beat. "No."

They finish the rest of the dishes without talking. Chris dries off his hands, turns around, and leans back against the counter, arms crossed. "So, what say you—in the unlikely event that this thing makes it over here, would you be okay with me inviting your lolo to move in with us?"

"How does it make you feel when you think about that possibility?" Enzo asks instead of answering, a technique he picked up from his therapist, Dr. Mendoza.

Chris's eyes wander to the ceiling as he scratches under his chin. "What will be, will be."

"Yeah, okay. Sure. But that's not an answer. What's coming up for you?"

"What do you mean?"

"Like, what emotions?"

Chris shrugs but says nothing. Enzo is disappointed but not surprised. They can talk about nearly anything in the world—so long as they stay on the surface.

"I may not be his biggest fan," Enzo says, letting Chris off the hook, "but if the other choice is to let him stay somewhere where he might catch a deadly virus, then . . . yeah, sure, I guess I'm okay with it." He sighs. "Utang na loob, right?"

Utang na loob: a debt from within. From the heart. It is a debt you did not ask for and will never pay off but must always try to. It is gratitude for the ancestors who brought you into existence, for the family who raised you, for the community who helped you in ways direct and indirect, visible and invisible. It is acknowledgment that none of us are alone.

For those who left, it is remittances. It is balikbayan boxes. It is dona-

14

tions after every typhoon, every eruption. It is massive multilingual family group chats. It is saying yes to being ninong or ninang to children you've never met. It is flying across the world for weddings and funerals and worrying about the savings account or credit cards later. It is the shame of missing weddings and funerals because the savings account is empty and the credit cards have reached their limit.

It is beautiful. It is burdensome.

It is the glue of community, the weight of obligation.

Chris also sighs. Nods. "Utang na loob."

MURDER HORNETS

"Are they murder hornets?" Dr. Mendoza asks Enzo a couple weeks later during their next session. Enzo has just shared the two things he hasn't been able to stop thinking about since they last met: this virus Dr. Young told his dad about, and the possibility of his lolo moving in with his family.

Murder hornets are a metaphor, of course. At their first meeting four years ago—when Enzo was twelve—Dr. Mendoza had asked him to describe what he physically felt like when he was anxious. Enzo had no idea what to say. Nobody had ever asked him to articulate the sensation. He thought on it, though, and had an answer ready to go the next time he sat down on the therapist's couch: his anxiety was a hornet's nest. At any given moment, a thousand buzzing worries were weaving erratic paths around him. Looming tests or essay deadlines. A group chat between his friends he learned he wasn't part of. Hurtful words he regretted saying. Any number of tragedies in the headlines he couldn't do anything about. His future. The future. And everything in between.

If unchecked, it left him constantly stressed, dizzy, distracted to the point that he couldn't sleep, couldn't focus, couldn't even remember simple things like his phone number. All the while, his entire body would tense, waiting to be stung.

It got especially bad in the seventh grade for no apparent reason. That's when Enzo's mom took him out for sushi one night, shared how therapy had helped her manage her depression over the years, and suggested he give it a try. Enzo agreed and, after consultations with three therapists, decided he felt most comfortable with Dr. Mendoza, a youngish Dominican man with an old-timey beard who was multiracial like Enzo.

After getting to know Enzo a bit and the ways in which Enzo experienced his anxiety, Dr. Mendoza had suggested integrating some calming strategies, like breath work, listening to chill music, journaling, spending time outside, exercising, eating well, and even playing low-stakes/no-stakes video games, into his daily routine.

"You mean I can tell my parents you told me to buy *Stardew Valley*?"

"Sure," Dr. Mendoza said. "That game's mad relaxing."

"It worked," Enzo announced a couple sessions later, after the hornet's nest quieted to a low-level hum, a white noise, and he no longer felt like his entire body was tensed up all the time. "I'm fixed."

Dr. Mendoza smiled gently. "Remember, this isn't about 'fixing' you, Enzo. You don't need to be 'fixed.'"

"Yeah, okay. Sure. Then why do my parents want to pay for me to come talk to you every other week about all the ways I'm messed up?"

"You're not 'messed up.' Everyone needs to learn to notice, process, and understand their emotions in a healthy way so they can heal. And since you struggle with anxiety, you also come here to learn tools for managing those specific feelings. So while I'm glad you found those strategies helpful, they're just the beginning. Big fish swim in deeper waters. You feel me?"

"I do not."

Dr. Mendoza explained what he meant. About how self-care alone is not enough. About developing the tools to unlearn unhealthy patterns. About exploring the ways we've been impacted by our families or the past or toxic systems in society. About how, in some cases, carefully tuned medication can help alongside all this other work. About how things often get worse before they get better.

Sure enough, every now and then, a worry would emerge from the hive, white-hot, vibrating a hundred times more intensely than the others, flying in to fuck shit up. A racist comment from a classmate he let slide. An argument between his parents that made him fear they were on the verge of divorce. Another school shooting that made him scared his school was next. And so on.

In these cases, no amount of breathing exercises or journaling or tree gazing would help. Enzo just had to accept it, talk through it with Dr. Mendoza, endure the ways it rattled his life, and wait for it to pass.

Enzo never had the perfect way to describe these particular periods of intense anxiety until this past fall, when he came across an article on social media about how scientists found a species of giant hornets living in the Pacific Northwest whose stings were supremely painful. "Murder hornets," the internet began to call them, and Enzo found his metaphor.

"Are they murder hornets?" Enzo says, repeating his therapist's question as his eyes go to the framed poster of the wheel of emotions that hangs on the wall behind Dr. Mendoza's chair. "I don't know. Not yet. Maybe soon? So, murder hornet larvae?"

Dr. Mendoza nods knowingly and waits for Enzo to say more.

"Like the thing with my lolo. It's not definite he's moving in with us— I'm not even sure he would if it really came down to it. So I guess there's no reason to worry about it yet. But if he did, it would be a massive dumpster fire because of how him and my dad are."

"Have you been talking this through with your dad?"

"Ha. Not really."

"Remember to keep the door open," Dr. Mendoza encourages.

"Sure, Doc. And in terms of the virus," Enzo goes on, "there's not much online beyond the fact it causes pneumonia in some people and that the 'authorities' are 'monitoring it.' Logically, then, I shouldn't worry about that either. It's probably nothing, they say. A blip."

"And yet?"

"And yet."

And yet.

The virus spreads. Within the month, people begin dying. A Chinese doctor in Wuhan who's in critical care after contracting the virus warns the world it's worse than his government claims—then dies. Confirmed cases are reported in several other countries, including the United States.

By the end of January, Enzo's dad calls Lolo Emil.

By mid-February, Lolo Emil agrees to move in.

Aligning Planets

It's late February and unseasonably warm. Leafless trees line the street. Enzo and Julia sit side by side at the top of their West Philly stoop as the sun rises over the skyline. Enzo's bent forward, elbows on knees. Julia's leaning back, a steaming mug of coffee on the step next to her. Enzo's dad should be arriving with Lolo Emil at any moment.

"Your dad and I appreciate you giving up your room," she says.

Enzo nods as if he actually had a choice. His parents did ask, but Julia uses the third bedroom as her home office, so that was never an option.

"Dad and Lolo Emil are going to kill each other, aren't they?" he asks.

Julia takes a sip from her coffee. "Maybe. Or maybe this will be good for them. Whenever we visit, it's never long enough for them to talk about anything real. To work through any of their issues."

"Yeah, I think that's on purpose."

"I suspect you're right."

"They're going to kill each other."

Julia rests her head on Enzo's shoulder. "Your dad's come a long way, Enzo."

"True," Enzo says. "But he still bottles everything up."

Julia sighs because she knows her son is right. The anger's still there, coursing under the surface. Chris has never been violent, and he stopped raising his voice years ago. Instead he grows suddenly silent and cold—then checks out for the next few days. It doesn't happen often, but it happens every time they visit Lolo Emil.

A young woman walks past with a small dog that resembles a fox. A trash truck rumbles down the street. Their next-door neighbor Ms. Li comes out, nods to them, and peers at the sky as if scanning for rain before ducking back inside her house.

"Here they come," Julia says a few moments later as the family's white Prius appears at the other end of the street.

Enzo looks up, takes a deep breath, and makes the sign of the cross. His mom swats the back of his head playfully.

As the car approaches, Enzo waves, his dad nods, and his grandfather glares. For a brief moment, three generations of Maghabol men align like planets. They share the same round face, wide nose, and warm brown eyes. In everything else—hair, height, body type, skin color—they're gradients of one another.

There's no parking out front, so the moment passes as they continue down the street in search of an open spot.

"Ay," Enzo's mom says, standing and stretching. "Your dad already looks upset. They must've already gotten into it. You ready for this?"

"No. You?"

She laughs. "No."

A few minutes later, Chris and Lolo Emil walk around the corner, arms loaded with luggage. And to Enzo's surprise, there's a dog trotting alongside them. It looks like a black Lab, but it must be mixed with something else because it's smaller than most other black Labs and has a tuft of white fur on its chest.

Enzo smiles and turns to his mom. Maybe this won't be all bad. "I didn't know he got a dog."

"Neither did I." She mutters something in Spanish under her breath that Enzo doesn't catch—some curse, he figures, since she's never been a dog person—then she puts on a smile and greets Lolo Emil with a kiss to each cheek.

"Julia," he says, pronouncing it the English way, as usual. "Good to see you again." He's clearly uncomfortable with the physical affection but endures it, then turns to Enzo and shakes his hand with a crushing grip. "Eric. You've grown about a foot since the last time I saw you. What are you now, fourteen?"

"Sixteen, Lolo. And I actually started going by 'Enzo' a few years ago."

Lolo Emil raises an eyebrow.

"*Enrique Lorenzo*," Enzo explains. "En. Zo."

Lolo Emil turns to Chris. "Are you going to let him put that on a résumé?"

"He'll put whatever name he wants, Dad," Chris says.

Lolo Emil shakes his head. "Well, I'm still going to call you Eric. That's a proper name. But while we're on the subject, quit it with the 'Lolo' business. We live in America. Call me 'Grandpa.'"

"Um, okay," Enzo says, deciding that he will call Lolo Emil "Grandpa" when Lolo Emil calls him "Enzo."

Lolo Emil turns his attention to the house, looking it up and down. "I thought you were going to upgrade, Christopher."

Chris takes a deep breath. "I told you, we don't need to upgrade, Dad. The house is perfect for us."

Lolo Emil scoffs. "A proper house should have a guest room, more than one bathroom, a dishwasher. . . . But at least you didn't buy across the river over in Whitman."

Julia's forced smile slides into a sneer. She grew up in Whitman.

"Can I pet your dog?" Enzo asks, eager to change the subject.

Lolo Emil nods. "This is Thor."

"Hi, Thor." Enzo kneels and the dog rushes over, tongue lolling out to one side as he leans against Enzo's legs. "How long have you had him?"

"About three years."

"And he never thought to mention him," Chris mumbles. Because like Julia, Chris is also not a dog person. Hence the reason they've always shut down Enzo's requests to get one over the years.

"He's a good boy." Enzo scratches Thor behind his ears. "How old?"

"Nine or ten, maybe. Don't know for sure. His muzzle was already gray when I adopted him from the shelter."

"He better be house-trained," Chris says.

"I've already told you that he is, Christopher."

"Good." And with that clever retort, Chris disappears into the house.

"Here," Julia says, reaching for one of Emil's suitcases, "let me help you with your things. Get you settled in."

"Nonsense." He nods toward Enzo. "The boy can carry them."

The boy.

Julia's smile falters. "Sure. Enzo, help your lolo."

Hoping this will not be a long visit, Enzo takes the bags and begins lugging them up the steps and into the house. He wonders what's inside—they're heavier than he expects.

Much heavier.

CHRIS

October 1983
Denver, CO

A BROKENNESS BEYOND REPAIR

Chris whips his rod forward, casting into the river. As the reel whirs, his fly arcs through the air and hits the water with a small splash, trailed by the softly coiling line, thin as a strand of silk.

"You overspooled again," says his dad, Emil, who's sitting on the bank in his waders, sunglasses, and hat, still sharpening his hooks.

Chris nods as he ignores the pain in his right shoulder from a massive hit he took from that lineman at last night's game. With freezing fingers, he picks up the slack before his line snags on a rock or stick. Around him, the river cuts through the surrounding mountains, flowing slow, low, and clear, shimmering as its rippling surface catches the sunlight.

It's a cold, crisp October morning bursting with greens and browns and oranges and yellows. Chris's breath puffs out in white clouds that float up toward the wide, deep blue Colorado sky as the water carries his fly downstream. No bite; he reels it in.

"Don't overcast," Emil says without looking. "Keep the fly on the water."

Chris says nothing as he recasts. Anything other than a *Yes, sir* would be back talk.

Emil tucks away the hook sharpener and stands. He assesses the river and selects a fly. He ties it on. He walks upstream. He casts.

So as not to spook the fish, they do not speak. There is the gentle rushing of the water. The rhythmic whip and whir of their rods and lines. The rustling of the turning leaves in the wind and the periodic splashing of a trout fighting for its life.

◆

Emil catches more than Chris, as usual. And as their day ends and they pack up, Emil explains why in elaborate detail. Chris nods at all the right moments, glad to be finished. This is probably one of their last Saturdays out before winter hits, if not the last. Chris enjoys being out in the mountains enough to tolerate his dad's unending criticism disguised as paternal wisdom, but Friday nights during football season have been kicking his butt and making it difficult to wake up at the crack of dawn to freeze his ass off and kill other living beings.

They peel off their waders, load their gear into the truck bed, and climb into the cab. Emil starts the engine, and the radio comes to life, playing that annoying country song "American Made."

"Best song I've heard in a long time," Emil says, as he does every time it comes on.

Chris would much rather pop in that new Run-D.M.C. cassette tape, but he's pretty sure his dad's head would explode. There's no point in even trying to change the station, so instead Chris reaches over to crank up the heat only to have Emil block his hand.

"We have to let her warm up first," he says.

Chris withdraws and exhales. A little too loudly.

Eyes forward, Emil clenches the steering wheel. "Okay. What's with the attitude, mister?"

Chris slouches, crosses his arms, and gazes out the window at the snowcapped stony peaks looming in the near distance beyond the mountainside carpeted in changing leaves. He tucks away his anger. "Sorry. Tired, is all. From the game."

Emil nods, shifts the truck into gear, and pulls away from the river, gravel crunching beneath the rolling tires. When they reach the paved road, he turns down the radio and says, "I've been thinking about that— you playing football, that is."

Chris's heart begins beating faster, bracing for yet another argument. "You said I could play this year."

"I did—as long as you're keeping your grades up."

"I have been." Chris focuses on a contrail slowly cutting through the perfect blue sky.

"So far. But if being on the team's already making you this tired, it's only a matter of time before that starts negatively impacting your school-work. We don't want a repeat of last year."

Chris does not need to be reminded of his freshman year. He had been excited to join the football team, but Emil refused to let him do so. Claimed it was a waste of time and that he needed to focus on his academics.

What followed was a year of missing assignments and incompletes and tests returned face down. Of detentions and lectures. Of no TV or Walkman or phone or sports or friends or fun. Of shame and shame and shame. A year of questions he could not answer—at least not honestly.

Why are you so lazy?

Why can't you be more like your sister?

Why don't you care about your future?

Are you on drugs?

What's wrong with you?

A year of his dad towering over him, arms crossed, fists clenched. *We give you everything that you need, Christopher. So many opportunities. But you waste them all. Is this what you want to be for the rest of your life: a disappointment?*

A year of downcast eyes, mouth shut. Of words smoldering somewhere out of reach in the pit of his belly. Of tears held back and anger held in because to release either would make things so much worse. Of hands that reached out claiming to help, only to hold him underwater.

In their minds, he was broken.

Their job was to fix him.

If they could not, then his was a brokenness beyond repair.

These were the messages his parents and teachers delivered, both explicitly and implicitly. Messages that fixed themselves firmly to his mind, shining bright as false stars.

The family had to cancel their annual summer road trip so Chris could attend summer school. But before it started, he proposed a deal to his parents: If he earned all As in his summer classes, they had to let him join the football team in the fall.

Emil, thinking this outcome was highly unlikely but hoping it would at least motivate Chris enough to scrape by, agreed. His stipulation: If Chris succeeded, he had to maintain a B average throughout the semester to *remain* on the team. Chris accepted. They shook.

And then Chris earned all As in his summer classes.

Because he was not lazy or disorganized or dumb or unmotivated.

His brain was not addled by drugs; his judgment, not impaired by bad friends.

He was not broken.

"You did it on purpose, didn't you?" asked his perfect younger sister, Amy, after his summer school report card arrived in the mail. "You self-sabotaged so you could come up with that football deal."

Chris smirked.

Amy laughed. "You little shit."

After all of that, now here is Emil, suggesting Chris quit the team as they drive home. All because Chris is tired from last night's game. Never mind the fact that he basically never stepped off the field. Or that they woke up before dawn to fish the river. Or that his grades are still fine. It's just an excuse to go back on their deal because his dad despises what he can't control.

I'm not quitting, Chris thinks as they come down the mountain. Aloud, he says, "Okay, Dad."

Emil makes that condescending *hmm* sound he always makes, then falls quiet. They drive the rest of the hour and a half home in silence.

When Chris was a kid, he loved riding shotgun in the middle of the night on their summer family road trips as his dad drove and his mom and sisters slept in the back. There was something sacred about oldies turned low on the radio, the highway humming under the tires, and city lights sliding past in the dark. No need to speak.

But this silence is different. Over the years, it has sharpened, grown teeth. Now neither can say a word that will not draw blood.

ON YOUR WAY

Fourth quarter. Down by three. Twenty-six seconds left. Chris's team has the ball on the thirty-seven yard line. Jason Larsen just threw two incomplete passes, so now it's third down.

The first snow of the year is falling, dusting the field and the players' helmets under the floodlights. The crowd's roaring, the marching band's blaring, the cheerleaders are chanting. It's so loud, Chris can barely hear Larsen call the next play in the huddle. But before he can ask him to repeat it, Larsen barks, "Ready . . ." and everyone responds, "Break!" as they clap in unison, then scramble to their positions.

Heart pounding, muscles vibrating, Chris is praying he heard the play right, when Dominic Moore, their fullback, slaps Chris's helmet and says, "Don't fuck this up, Gonzales." Chris nods as he lines up behind Moore.

Chris glances up into the bleachers to his right. His best friend, Hazel Young, one of the few Black students in the mostly white crowd, is shouting as she waves their school's pennant. A few rows up from her, Chris's family. His mom and sisters are clapping and cheering with the rest of the bundled-up fans, but his dad's arms are crossed over his chest, his mouth set in a grim line.

As the linemen drop into three-point stances, Chris brings his focus back to the game. A tense stillness settles over the field. Larsen sets up behind the center, hands open, and begins calling his cadence. Across the line of scrimmage, the middle linebacker that knocked Chris flat on his ass in the third quarter glares at him like a starving mountain lion.

"Hut!" Larsen finally calls, and the world bursts into motion.

Chris charges forward. Larsen fakes the handoff to Moore, then shoves the ball into Chris's stomach. A pair of linemen lunge for Moore, opening a crack in the middle of the line. Chris slips through, spins, cuts left, jukes right, cuts left again. Everything is a blur, but Chris weaves through the melee, swings out to the sideline, and sprints up the open field at full speed.

Nobody can catch him, not even the safety, and he sails into the end zone as the clock runs down. He drops the ball and raises his hands in victory. His team crashes into him. The home crowd rushes the field. In the crush of high fives and helmet slaps and back pats, Chris reaches for his people. He finds Hazel Young first and wraps his arms around her. He finds his sisters and his mom next and embraces them as well. But when Chris pulls away, there's no sign of Emil.

"Where's Dad?" he asks his family, shouting to be heard.

"He went to warm up the car!" his mom shouts back.

"What?" Chris says, because he definitely didn't hear what he thinks he heard. Not right now. Not after *that* play.

She cups her hands around her mouth and repeats, "He went to warm up the car!"

Amy gives him a sympathetic shrug.

Before Chris can respond, his teammates hoist him up onto their shoulders. They carry him away toward the locker room, chanting, "Speedy! Speedy! Speedy!" as he looks back at his family, face falling.

*

It's still snowing lightly when Chris and his teammates finally emerge from the locker room. Hazel is leaning against the wall by the parking lot in her black peacoat and matching red scarf and cap knitted by her mom, reading a book held open in gloved hands.

"Hey, Hazel," Chris says.

Hazel looks up and smiles. "Finally."

His teammates flow past, heading to their vehicles. "Let me guess," Chris says, "they asked if I could catch a ride with you?"

She brushes snowflakes from the page and closes the book. "Your dad wanted to beat the rush."

Chris takes his beanie out, pulls it on, and joins Hazel against the wall. "Of course he did."

"My dad should be here soon, though."

Chris nods. Then someone plucks Chris's hat off his head and tousles his hair. It's Larsen and, next to him, Moore.

"Great job, Gonzales!" Larsen says, grinning. Then he holds out the hat to hand it back.

"Thanks," Chris says, and reaches for it.

But Larsen pitches it to Moore, who sprints away, raises his hands in victory, and spikes Chris's beanie onto the damp cement as if he's just scored an imaginary touchdown. Larsen jogs to catch up with Moore, and the two walk away, laughing.

"Dicks," Hazel says under her breath.

"They're cool." Chris retrieves his hat.

"You just won the game for them."

"They're only messing with me."

"Right. Like how they're still pulling that racist shit and calling you 'Speedy Gonzales'?"

Chris shrugs. "It's not racist. It's just a nickname."

"I bet they don't even know your real last name. Or that you're part Filipino, not part Mexican."

Chris pops his coat collar. "Whatever."

They watch as people brush snow off windshields, start engines, click on headlights, and drive away.

"Oh, speaking of which," Hazel says after a few minutes, "you meet the new girl yet?"

"What new girl?"

"The one from the Philippines? She's a senior, I think."

Chris gestures to the falling snow. "Someone moved from a tropical paradise to *here*?"

"Yeah."

"No way," he says. He's never gone to school with another Filipino student other than his sisters.

"Yes way."

"But why?"

Hazel shrugs. "Ask her yourself."

"What's her name?"

"Rebecca something."

Chris laughs. "'Rebecca' isn't a very Filipino name."

Hazel side-eyes Chris. "Oh, I didn't realize that you know everyone's name in the Philippines."

"I'm just saying."

Hazel shakes her head. "And I'm just saying that was an ignorant comment. Like, you're 'Chris,' and your sisters are 'Amy' and 'Jenny.'"

"Yeah, but we're only half."

"There he is," Hazel says, and punches Chris's shoulder as her dad's car comes into sight. They push off the wall and step up to the curb, leaving shallow footprints melting in their wake. "By the way, you should say something to your dad."

Chris shifts the bag slung over his shoulder. "About what?"

"About how it sucked that he didn't stick around to say 'good job' or give you a hug or nod meaningfully from a distance or something."

"I don't care."

"It doesn't bother you? Like, at all?"

Chris shakes his head as Mr. Young's car pulls up. "That's just how he is. He's not like your dad, okay?"

"If you say so." Hazel reaches for the passenger door, but the car rolls forward a few feet. Hazel tries again, but the car drives just out of reach a second time. Hazel sighs. Tries again. This time the car stays put.

Mr. Young is cracking up behind the wheel as Hazel and Chris step out of the cold, snowy night and into the warmth and Motown that fill his car's interior.

"Real funny, Dad," Hazel says.

"Classic, Mr. Young," Chris says.

Hazel rolls her eyes, buckles her seat belt, turns down the radio. "Yeah, a classic butt."

"Ignore her," Mr. Young tells Chris. "I can use all the validation I can get. But enough about me—how'd the game go?"

Hazel tells her dad all about it. When she gets to Chris's winning touchdown, he makes eye contact with Chris in the rearview mirror, beaming, and gives him a fist bump between the front seats. "Well, look at that—we've got the next Tony Dorsett back here! Maybe I should get your autograph before you start charging!"

"It was a lucky play," Chris says, looking away. "I'm not that good."

"You're on your way, son," Mr. Young says. "And someday I'll be telling everyone how you used to bum free rides off me."

Chris's smile doesn't escape Hazel's notice. "Christopher Maghabol," she says, "you care."

"About what?" Mr. Young asks.

"Nothing," Chris says, smile fading as he shifts in his seat. "Nothing."

Hazel rolls her eyes. "If you say so."

THE MAN OF THE HOUSE

"What do you mean, I'm off the team?" Chris says. He's in Coach's cramped office in the corner of the locker room as everybody else gears up for practice, halfway changed himself.

Coach sits at his desk behind a mountain of papers, forms, and playbooks. Arms crossed over his chest, he clears his throat and leans back in his chair. "Exactly that."

Chris shakes his head in stunned disbelief. Anger and confusion swirl within his chest like a gathering storm. He hadn't missed a single practice or slacked off for even a second, even when he had the flu last week. Sure, he hadn't scored a touchdown in two games, but he'd been racking up decent rushing yards, and he'd caught a few interceptions on defense.

Chris's eyes drift to the dusty trophies crowding the top of a filing cabinet behind Coach. "What'd I do wrong?"

"Nothing. This isn't about you as a player, Gonzales. You've been impressing the hell out of all of us. Especially for a rookie sophomore." Coach uncrosses his arms, adjusts his hat, and leans back. The vent in the corner rattles as it blows hot air into the room. "It's your old man—he doesn't want you playing anymore."

Chris lets out an angry chuckle. "Of course not." He shakes his head some more. "Did he even say why?"

"Your grades."

"What about them? They're fine."

"You're eligible by the athletic department's standards—but not by his, it seems. Said something about a missing essay for your history class?"

Chris opens his mouth to call his dad a liar—but then closes it. Shit. *That* paper. Something about personal ancestry. It was due last week, but he couldn't think of anything to write about, and then he'd been so out of it between getting sick and not wanting to miss school or practice, it had completely slipped his mind. His teacher must have called home about it today.

"I'll talk to Ms. Pérez," Chris says. "She'll let me turn it in late. I know she will."

"Be that as it may, you still have to speak to your father."

"I will. Tonight. I promise."

Coach nods. "Good."

"So I can practice today?"

Coach shakes his head. "Sorry, Gonzales. If your father doesn't want you stepping onto that field, you can't step onto that field until he tells me otherwise. He's the man of the house, and you've got to respect that. What he says goes. End of story."

Chris lets out an exasperated sigh. "This is bullshit."

"Language, Gonzales."

"Sorry, Coach," Chris says, slumping in the chair as his anger melts into mourning. He'd finally found something he was really good at— something he loved—and his dad just had to snatch it away.

Coach nods, then stands. "There's always next season." He pulls on his jacket, scoops his whistle and clipboard off his desk, and claps Chris on the shoulder on his way out. "Give him some time. I'm sure he'll come around."

"Sure, Coach," Chris says, wishing he could believe that, wishing he could for once in his life say what he truly feels.

EMIL

May 1965
Stockton, CA

THE SUBIC BAY CAFÉ

Emil Maghabol is refilling the saltshakers at the Subic Bay Café, which sits at the corner of Lafayette and El Dorado, between the Aklan Hotel and the Bataan Pool Hall, opposite the Lafayette Lunch Counter and the Farm Workers Union. The intersection is the beating heart of the four square blocks of brick storefronts that comprise downtown Stockton's Little Manila.

Soon the Filipino laborers will pour into the café after a day of cutting asparagus on one island or another in the San Joaquin Delta. They will bask in scents and sounds that remind them of home. They will check their reflections in the mirror behind the counter, then check the shoebox on the counter for their mail. They will slide into seats, light cigarettes, and lean back. They will eat dinuguan or hotcakes, adobo or hamburgers, and drink a San Mig—or two or three—while exchanging tips about jobs or swapping gossip in Ilokano, Visayan, or Tagalog.

But for now it is just Emil and his auntie Carmen up front. Late-afternoon sunlight streams in through the street-facing windows, casting long shadows across the booths, as Emil preps the place for the dinner rush and Auntie Carmen sits at the counter smoking a cigar and reading the paper.

She and her husband, Emil's uncle Tony, bought the place almost twenty years ago—four years before Emil was born. When Emil was ten,

Uncle Tony passed away, and Emil began helping out. When he turned thirteen, Auntie Carmen began paying him. Since his father is rarely around and his mother is always working at the hotel, it is where Emil spends most of his life when not in class. Where he eats, studies, learns about the world.

Every day after school and most of the weekends, he chops vegetables, brews coffee, buses tables, empties ashtrays, refills condiment and napkin holders, takes out garbage bag after garbage bag, mops floors, washes windows and dishes, scrubs pots and pans, scrapes the grill, cleans the bathroom, makes soap from excess fat, and does whatever else needs to be done that his auntie or cousins prefer not to do.

Hard work, but honest and better than the fields. The biggest downside: The diners are forever asking where they can find Emil's father, Francisco. Emil, however, doesn't usually know—or care. He shrugs with practiced indifference and focuses on whatever task is at hand.

"Another failed farmworkers' strike," Auntie Carmen says in English shaking her head at an article in the way she does when revving up for one of her rants. "They're asking for a forty-cent raise! Forty cents! Can you imagine? That's nearly half of what they're making now. It's absolute nonsense. Of course what they do is hard work. Of course they don't make as much as the whites or even the Mexicans. What do they expect? They knew what they were getting into when they came here. Yet all they do now is complain. All the manongs should consider themselves lucky to have been let in before the door closed in '34. They had the opportunity to make more money than they could have ever made back in their provinces, the chance to gain a foothold for themselves. If they didn't want to grow old in those fields, then they shouldn't have spent all their money on zoot suits and white women!"

Half listening since he's heard it all before, Emil nods as he moves from one booth to the next.

Auntie Carmen folds the paper closed, slaps it onto the counter, and swivels the stool around to face Emil. "I love the man—he's my big brother after all—but I don't get why he and his Commie friends are always stirring up trouble. The growers will never pay them more. And why should they, ha? They were never supposed to hold these jobs forever. That's like clinging to the bottom rung of the ladder and arguing that it should be wider instead of climbing higher. They need to earn their place in this country, prove that they deserve to be here so they can move up. It's not difficult to understand." She points her cigar at Emil. "There are a hundred men looking for work on every street corner. You want to make something of yourself, boy? Be one of a kind. Irreplaceable."

"Yes, Auntie."

Auntie Carmen snubs out the cigar in an ashtray, then crosses her arms over her chest. "You want to be successful, look to men like your uncle Tony, God rest his soul. He worked hard. Became a contractor. Saved. Fought for this country to earn citizenship. And as soon as that Japanese family was gone, seized the opportunity to buy this place. Went from field hand to businessman like that." She snaps. "And just you wait, soon enough your cousins—not Leon, but the others—will go off to college and land careers I could only dream of. Be like that, Emil. Not like your father."

Emil nods as he screws the lid back onto a shaker, clenching his jaws as he braces for his auntie's familiar—but fair—criticisms of Francisco.

"Blacklisted by every grower in town. Kicked out of the United Sons.

Depending on his widowed sister to feed and house his wife and child."
She ticks off each offense on a finger. "And don't forget nearly getting us
all deported."

The door chimes as it swings open. In saunters Auntie Gia, whose husband owns the dry cleaner a few doors down. She's grinning in the way
she always does when she's got gossip trapped behind her teeth.

"Guess who's back in town?" she calls out in singsongy Ilokano.

"English," Auntie Carmen gently admonishes as she nods toward Emil.
He understands Ilokano but stopped speaking it years ago at her behest.

"Ay, sorry," Auntie Gia says, switching languages as she covers her
mouth in mock shame. She takes a seat at the counter next to Auntie Carmen, slips a cigarette from a pack she pulls from her purse, and holds it
out in the air. Emil stops what he's doing and lights it. "As I was saying,
guess who's found the time to grace us with his presence?"

"Just tell us, Gia," Auntie Carmen says.

"You're never any fun." Auntie Gia pouts. She takes a drag from her
cigarette and then slowly blows out the smoke to draw out suspense
nobody asked for. Finally she raises her eyebrow and points at Emil with
her lips.

"Francisco?" Auntie Carmen asks.

Auntie Gia nods.

Emil gets back to work, mixed feelings settling into the pit of his stomach. He's grown accustomed to Francisco's absences, and his life's easier
in a lot of ways when the man isn't around. Yet as much as he pretends
otherwise, there's a part of him that remains excited at the possibility of
seeing his father after nearly a month. Not as big a part as when he was
little but a part nonetheless. A sliver. A seed waiting for water.

"He came by our place this morning," Auntie Gia goes on.

"So he's done in Coachella Valley, ha?" Auntie Carmen says.

"Guess so. With our asparagus season ending, he's trying to convince everyone else to go with him to Delano next to join Mang Larry. Including my Eddie."

Emil deflates. Of course his father did not return for his family. And of course his father won't be staying long. Delano's over two hundred miles to the south.

"But Mang Eddie isn't even a field-worker," Auntie Carmen notes.

"Right. Apparently Mang Isko's speaking to *all* the men, whether or not they're in the fields anymore. He says this is going to be a big one. That he's even been talking to that Mexican woman—Dolores what's-her-name."

Auntie Carmen shrugs.

"Well, he's been talking to her and that white priest to convince the Mexicans to join."

Auntie Carmen sighs with disapproval. "Don't tell me he convinced Eddie to go? I know my brother can be persuasive, always acting the part of the hero—"

"Almost." Auntie Gia scoffs. "But I knocked sense into him. He's an old man already. He has a family. Owns a business and a home. Why would he go argue about wages for a job he doesn't have in some town where he doesn't live? I'll be damned if he's going to leave me to run the cleaners and take care of the kids all alone so he can go help a bunch of fools who are just going to end up getting fired."

"Or blacklisted," Auntie Carmen says.

"Or killed," Auntie Gia adds, eyes widening in exaggerated fear, "like that Black fellow in New York who was always so angry about every-thing."

"See?" Auntie Carmen says to Emil. "Best not to rock the boat."

"Yes, Auntie," Emil says.

"And that's not all," Auntie Gia says, having saved the juiciest piece of gossip for last.

Auntie Carmen and Emil wait for Auntie Gia to go on, but the woman takes another long drag from her cigarette, savoring the silence of anticipation.

"Out with it already," Auntie Carmen says.

But Auntie Gia clears her throat and nods toward Emil, not as subtly as she might think.

"Ah," Auntie Carmen says, then turns to Emil. "The vegetables aren't going to chop themselves, ha? Your kuya Leon will need to start cooking soon as he returns."

"Yes, Auntie," Emil responds. The women wait silently as he screws on the lid of the last saltshaker, wipes the stray crystals from the countertop, and heads to the back. But as soon as he's through the sheet that's draped across the doorway to separate the dining room from the kitchen, he stops and listens as they resume their conversation in Ilokano.

"You going to make me wait all day?" Auntie Carmen says.

"I need you to promise not to tell anyone," Auntie Gia says.

"Spit it out already."

"Fine, fine, fine." Auntie Gia pauses as if gathering herself. "Rumor has it . . ."

But whatever secret Auntie Carmen divulges, she shares too quietly for Emil to catch. The next thing he hears is Auntie Carmen tutting for a long time to convey deep, deep disapproval.

"Wish I could say that surprises me," she says eventually. "I'll talk to him."

"Good."

"Enough about my brother. Let's discuss something else."

Their conversation turns to the ongoing highway construction and how the destruction of the West End will be worth it when it revitalizes the downtown like the redevelopment agency says it will. Emil couldn't care less. He turns away and makes his way over to the sink. He plugs the drain, opens the tap, and lets the sound of the rushing water wash out his wondering about whatever Auntie Gia revealed.

Why does his father refuse to work his way up? At the very least, why doesn't he stay quiet? Instead it's organize, unionize, mobilize, educate, petition, protest, strike, boycott, and so forth. It never ends. Why does he have to fight every fight? And for what? Even when it seems like the ideas are taking, the workers almost always change their minds as soon as the growers threaten to fine or fire or arrest or deport. Or, when they don't, the growers hire thugs to swing bats and fists and crowbars to ensure the strike or boycott does not last.

Either way, the results are always the same:

Failure.

Shame.

More trouble.

Trouble for Francisco, whose jobs last only until the grower hears about what he is up to. Trouble for their family, who's still stuck sharing a shitty apartment with near strangers. Trouble for Emil, who goes to school with the growers' children. Trouble for all the Filipinos who will pay for the actions of a few.

When Emil succeeds, it will be despite his father.

Isang bagsak, he imagines his father saying in disagreement. It's the phrase they shout at his meetings, what the man always says when someone tries to talk some sense into him. His claim that they are all in this together, that they will rise or fall as one.

It's baloney, of course.

Everyone is on their own, like Auntie Carmen always says. Crabs in a barrel, fighting and climbing one another to escape. The Americans understand this deeply. It's the rugged individualism of the frontier, the fierce competition of capitalism. It may seem harsh, but it breeds strength. It's how the US became the most powerful country on Earth, the destination for all who want to build a better life and are willing to work for it. Wasn't that why his father came here to begin with? If America ever falls, it will be because of this creeping expectation that everything should be handed to people for free.

The sink finishes filling, so Emil closes the tap. He grabs a crate of misshapen tomatoes picked by hands as brown as his and tips it over, sending them splashing into the cold water. He rinses off the dirt that clings to their smooth ruby skin, then sharpens the knife and sets to dicing them into something useful as he braces himself for his father's return.

⮞

After his shift, Emil retreats to the two-bedroom apartment above the café, which his family used to share with Auntie Carmen's. But ever since her family bought the house in the south side, Emil and his parents have shared the place with a rotating cast of migrant laborers they call cousins or uncles, who are rarely literal cousins or uncles. On most nights the men stay up late drinking, smoking, listening to the Beatles while playing cards or mahjong, pulling Emil unwillingly into their arguments or games should he venture out of the room he shares with his parents.

Thankfully there's no sign of these cousins and uncles tonight. No sign of his mother. And no sign of his father—which makes Emil feel equal parts relief and disappointment.

Taking advantage of the quiet, Emil draws a bath and scrubs off the dirty dish stench that stains his skin. Afterward he slips on his pajamas, crushes a few cockroaches in the kitchen, then sits down at the small, wobbly table to finish his homework and review his notes by the orange light of the streetlamps that leak through the window. Since final exams are coming up, he only lets himself go to bed when he knows all the material forward and backward, when the facts are firmly committed to memory.

Because his auntie Carmen is right. He wants more than to waste his days stooped over in a field or hunched over a grill. More than a too-small apartment with too many people. More than a life of hard labor with nothing to show for it other than the four square blocks to which many of these aging manongs cling.

NOT LIKE THE OTHERS

The bell rings and students spring out of their seats, escaping into the hallways of Franklin High on their way to lunch. But Emil takes his time. It's not like he's meeting up with anyone.

Mrs. Briggs wanders over as he's still gathering his things. "Mr. Maghabol, can I speak to you for a moment?"

She says his last name like MAG-*uhble*, as if it rhymes with *drag-able*. He doesn't correct her. It's how everyone pronounces it. Maybe he'll change it someday.

"Yes, ma'am?" Emil says, giving his math teacher his full attention.

"It's about yesterday's exam."

Emil's heart stops. He must have failed it. But how? He had spent every extra minute he wasn't working at the café studying and had even stayed up nearly all night reviewing his notes and completing practice problems until he knew each concept through and through.

Mrs. Briggs's blue eyes widen when she notices his sudden panic. "Oh, I mean you did really well—a perfect score, actually! The only one in the class."

Relief washes over Emil. "Oh."

But why is she telling him this instead of letting him find out when she passes back the tests in ascending order of score like usual? Maybe she thinks he cheated. Does she think he cheated?

His mind's already working on how he might prove his innocence as she continues. "You're one of the strongest math students I've ever taught, and I even used to work over at Stockton High," she says, referring to the all-white school in the wealthy part of town. "Your mind is quick, analytical, persistent. Always searching for solutions, finding the patterns."

Okay, she doesn't think he cheated—she's complimenting him. He drops his gaze to the floor and clears his throat. "Um. Thank you, ma'am."

"But most importantly, you're very, very diligent. I see how closely you listen when I lecture, and your notes, your work—so neat and meticulous! Even your handwriting is impressively consistent!"

Emil warms, glad she's noticed. Most teachers don't. "Thank you, ma'am."

"Have you ever thought about a career in mathematics?"

"No, ma'am," he lies. He doesn't want to appear prideful.

"You most certainly should. With a mind and a work ethic like yours, you could be an engineer, an accountant, an investment broker, or something along those lines. You're not like the others, Emil—your future isn't in the fields."

Emil's heart glows white-hot, as white as the skin at Mrs. Briggs's throat. He wishes he could open his chest and show her. Or, at the very least, he wants to say thank you again—but three times seems boastful even if there's no higher compliment she could have paid him.

She goes on. "But I didn't just ask you to stay after so I can tell you what you probably already know. Rather, I have a practical proposal." Her smile widens. "I think you should skip ahead two levels next year."

"Really?" he asks, taken aback. "Two?"

"There's some work you'll need to do this summer, but I can lend you the textbooks you need. From what I've seen this past year, you'll have no problem working through the material on your own. You're exactly the kind of student who can handle the challenge."

Emil nods.

"The class is mostly seniors," she continues, "so you'd be the only junior and the only one of your kind there. Do you think it would be okay with your father, though? He'll have to sign a course approval form."

"Of course, ma'am," Emil says.

"Great!" Mrs. Briggs retrieves a paper from her desk and slides it in front of Emil. "Have your father sign it, then bring it back to me tomorrow. I'll let you run off to lunch now. Sorry to keep you from your friends!"

"It's no bother, ma'am," Emil says.

Mrs. Briggs shoots him one more smile before leaving.

Emil scans the form. Back in junior high, he had asked his father about taking an advanced math course. His father had lectured Emil against thinking he was so much better than everyone else because of his grades and how he needed to dedicate more time caring for their community instead of doing more homework. He refused to talk about it any further, and Emil never got to take the class.

Emil doesn't want to relive that experience and hasn't even seen Francisco despite the fact the man's been back in town a few days. So he forges his father's signature and slips the paper between the pages of his math book. Then he grabs the rest of his things and heads into the hallway.

But as soon as he exits the classroom, Emil's foot catches on something, and he trips forward. His books fly out of his hands, and he crashes onto the floor as laughter ripples through the hallway, extinguishing the glow of pride he had been feeling only a moment before.

"Oh, sorry," says Richard Murphy, one of the smirking white boys lingering in a clump by the nearby lockers. One of the growers' sons. "Didn't see you there."

Emil says nothing as he gathers his books and scrambles back to his feet. He says nothing as he walks away, even when Richard Murphy shouts at Emil to tell his Commie father to go back to his own country as Richard's friends howl like monkeys. What would be the point? Let them laugh now. He will laugh later when they all end up with mediocre jobs, stuck forever in this godforsaken town.

Emil's almost at the end of the hallway when he feels a light touch at his elbow. He jerks his arm away and picks up his pace. But the person doesn't give up so easily.

"You okay, Emilio?" they ask, walking fast alongside him.

Emil doesn't need to look to know it's Sammy Bautista. Junior-class vice president. Point guard on the varsity basketball team. Star of the glee club and photography club. And one of the most handsome Filipino boys in school. At least that's what the girls say. Probably because of his hair or something.

If it were anyone else, Emil would ignore them. But it's not, so he slows and tries to hide his anger and embarrassment. "I'm fine, thanks," he answers pointedly in English to preempt the inevitable taunting from their white classmates or the likely admonishments from their white teachers.

"Those guys are real jerks."

"Sure."

Sammy shakes his head. "It's supposed to be 1965, not 1935. Know what I mean?"

"Right."

"Want me to tell the principal or something?"

"Definitely not."

"Yeah, he probably wouldn't do anything anyway."

They keep walking. Emil tries to come up with a topic of conversation unrelated to his most recent humiliation, but before he can, Sammy saves him. "Forget about them. What are you doing right now?"

Emil scratches the back of his neck. "Right now?"

"Yeah, for lunch." Sammy smiles.

Emil casts a sideways glance at Sammy. The kid really does have great hair, Emil has to admit. "Um. I don't know."

"A few of us are meeting to talk about starting up a Filipino Student Union next year."

"Why?" Emil asks.

"We admire what the Black Student Union has been doing and think that it might be a good idea to organize something like that for our people."

Emil faces forward again, uninterested in giving Richard Murphy and his friends another reason to continue tormenting him. "I can't. Sorry."

"You sure? I figured that as the son of Francisc—"

"I have to study."

"Oh," Sammy says with the tender hurt of someone unaccustomed to rejection. "Maybe you can find us if you finish up early. We'll be in the quad."

Emil burns with anger at himself for thinking this was anything other than a half-assed club recruitment effort based solely on the fact he's the son of a man with a megaphone glued to his face.

He forces a smile. "Will do."

ISANG BAGSAK

It's not until Saturday night that Emil finally sees Francisco. As Emil climbs the stairs to their apartment after his shift, he smells the smoke and hears the muffled din of voices that are the telltale signs of a meeting. Emil considers going elsewhere, but there's nowhere else to go.

Sure enough, the living room is packed. People fill the chairs and line the walls, some as young as Emil, others as old as his lolo Carlos. They wait for the speeches to begin, talking among themselves as their calloused hands grip beers and balance plates and cradle cigarettes. On the muted TV set, the Dodgers are walloping the Senators at the top of the eighth inning.

Francisco is at the center of the crowd, of course, deep in conversation with Father McCullough and a couple of other men. Apparently Francisco's grown a patchy beard since the last time he was home. It does not look good.

Emil makes his way over to his mother, who's in the kitchen serving food and drinks, bags under her eyes from her own full day of work at the hotel and now this. "Hey, Ma," he says, kissing her on the cheek.

"Mi cielito lindo," she says, and wraps her arms around him. "Are you hungry?"

"I ate downstairs already," Emil says. "Think I'm just going to hit the hay."

"Make sure to say hi to your father first."

Emil glances over at Francisco. "He seems busy."

"He's eager to see you. Been asking after you all week."

"I'm sure he has," Emil says, and makes a beeline for the bedroom.

He's almost through the living room when Francisco shouts, "Emilio!"

"Presidente?" someone jokes, and everyone laughs.

Keeping his head down, Emil offers a small nod and keeps moving.

"Not that traitor, thankfully," Francisco says in Tagalog, making the room chuckle once more. Then he calls Emil's name again as he waves his son over.

Reluctantly, Emil goes. Francisco wraps him in a too-tight, too-long hug. When they pull apart, Francisco slips into English and introduces Emil to the men he'd been talking to, bragging about how he's at the top of his class.

If Emil's being honest with himself, the man's presence always softens some of the anger that has hardened in his absence. Doesn't every son long for his father's approval, like a plant bending toward light?

Switching to Ilokano, Francisco asks Emil, "We're about to get started—will you stay?"

The request—and the genuinely hopeful look in his eyes—catches Emil off guard. This is the first time in years his father has bothered to ask.

"I don't know," Emil answers in English. "Finals are coming up, and—"

"Please, anak. It would mean a lot to me."

Emil checks his watch. Sighs. "Fine."

Francisco breaks out into a wide smile and ruffles Emil's hair. Then he steps onto the coffee table and clears his throat theatrically. Eyes turn and conversations fall quiet as Francisco surveys the room. When the silence is complete, he gestures to Emil. "Come on up, anak."

Emil shakes his head, souring as he realizes why his father's asked him to stay.

"Please. By my side." And that smile again, that look of genuine hope.

All the manongs urge Emil onward, so he has no choice but to join his father on the table. Francisco claps a hand on Emil's shoulder. "This is what we're fighting for," he says, looking into Emil's eyes but addressing the room. "This. Our children."

"I don't have any children, Isko," one of the older manongs shouts in Kapampangan from the back of the room.

"Me neither," says another in Tagalog.

"That's because you're both too damn ugly to get any women!" someone says in English, and the room erupts in laughter.

When it subsides, Francisco addresses the crowd again, this time in the somber, resonant voice he uses for speeches. "My child is your child. Sonny's children are your children. Tony's children are your children." Francisco goes on, naming what seems like every father in the room, weaving effortlessly between languages. "And all the children down in Delano are your children. They are all your children. They are all our children. Because we are one community. One barangay. One province. One people. When any of us are in need, it doesn't matter where we hail from. We take care of each other, we fight for what we deserve, and we give our children what they need. Isang bagsak, di ba?"

Isang bagsak: One down. Or: One accomplishment, many more to go. Or: If one falls, we all fall. Or: If one rises, we all rise. Or: We are in this together.

Too bad it's horseshit, Emil thinks, squirming under his father's clammy grip as he drops his eyes to the floor. Sounds nice and all in a speech, but like Auntie Carmen always says, their children don't need men who spend their days in the fields, their nights in the pool halls, their weekends betting on cockfights. Men who complain about higher wages that they'd likely gamble or drink away. Men who define themselves by where they came from instead of where they could be.

No. They need men who work *and* work their way up. Disciplined men who save and go straight home after returning from the fields. Who read the real newspapers, obey this country's laws, and practice their English until their island accents disappear.

"This was the mindset of our ancestors that we must relearn," Francisco continues, unaware of his son shifting uneasily under his hand. "Isang bagsak. Kapwa. Bayanihan. Solidaridad. Whatever we know this value as, America has tried to make us forget how to practice unity. They want us to believe that it is every man for himself, that we must destroy each other to succeed. But who does this mindset benefit?"

"The growers!" a young man shouts with righteous indignation. A few others call out their agreement.

"Right!" Emil's father releases Emil's shoulder so he can gesture with both hands now. Emil edges away, free from his use as a prop but at the cost of being forgotten. "Because if we are only caring about ourselves, then we do not have power. If the Mexicans cut the grapes, the Filipinos pack the grapes, and the Blacks deliver the grapes, then we never talk, never see that our plight is the same. Because one voice alone is loud enough to thank the growers for scraps but not loud enough to demand a fair wage. One set of hands is strong enough to tend their crops but not our future. One pair of fists is powerful enough to fight for today but not for tomorrow."

Men clap and stomp and shout and whistle, the room now hanging on Francisco's every word. Emil steps down off the table and melts into the crowd. Francisco doesn't even notice.

Instead Francisco goes on, recounting the indignities and exploitations, the history and the victories of the Filipino labor struggles in the plantations and canneries and fields. Then he moves into the closing of his speech.

"Join me and Mang Larry down in Delano this fall," he says. "Fight with us for what is fair, what is right. Not just a raise but a real contract. Stand with us against the greedy grape growers down there just like many of you stood with us in our victory against the asparagus growers up here in '48 or in Coachella Valley just last week. Join your voices and your hands and your fists with those of your kailian so we can fight as one for true equality in this country."

As the crowd roars with approval and thrusts fists into the air, Emil slips into the bedroom and closes the door. He lies down on the fraying mattress, shuts his eyes, and covers his ears with his pillow.

The Richard Murphys of this country will never accept those who cling to the ways of their home countries, who refuse to adapt. How can you expect to be welcomed into a place when your heart isn't there? If they want to be Filipino, then they should return to the Philippines instead of complaining about their lives here while petitioning to bring over more family members. As Emil's history teacher once advised him— fully aware of the fact Emil was born in California—"If you want to be

American, act American. Act well enough, and eventually nobody will be able to tell the difference."

The walls and the pillow are not dense enough to silence the sound of the unity clap. As always, everyone brings their hands together in a quiet, slow, and steady rhythm—easy enough for Emil to ignore. But it's a heartbeat that builds. And builds. And builds. People begin to stomp in time, and soon the apartment rumbles with a thundering beat that gains speed as it grows in volume and intensity.

When it seems like the sound shakes not only the apartment but the entire block, everyone begins clapping rapidly, transforming the beat into a wave that won't stop crashing until, finally, over the deafening roar, Francisco shouts, "Isaaaaaaaaang bagsak!" and the group punctuates the call with a final, booming clap.

Then silence. Then the muffled shifting, laughter, and conversations of tension dissolving, the room relaxing.

Emil turns to his side so he's facing the window and settles in for sleep. It's not remotely quiet and the sound of the clapping still rings in his ears, but he expects no peace so long as his father is around.

FRANCISCO

November 1929
Watsonville, CA

HANDS

Francisco is working next to Mang Carlos again. The old-timer is forever squinting, forever singing Ilokano folk songs to himself through a mouth of crooked teeth. Even with a bent back and cracked hands, he moves faster than Francisco. What pain he holds he's learned to hide.

"Hoy, Isko," Mang Carlos calls from atop the ladder within the next tree as he cradles, twists, plucks apples from their branches.

"Wen Apo?" Francisco asks, as if he doesn't already know what comes next.

Mang Carlos raises his eyebrow and gestures with his lips toward the horizon. "There—that should be you."

Francisco looks out of respect, but it's the same thing he sees almost every weekday morning: In the distance, a group of white boys walking. Books in hand. No rush. The growers' sons on their way to school.

"Once you get your education and leave these fields," Mang Carlos says, "then you can marry one of my daughters!"

Francisco forces a smile. "How do your daughters feel about that?"

"Good point—your friend Lorenzo is much more handsome!"

"And taller," Francisco notes.

"And smarter!" adds Lorenzo, his voice floating through the leaves of a nearby tree.

Although many of the old-timers like to tease the younger men by offering up hypothetical daughters, Mang Carlos is one of the few with a family and one of the even fewer with a family who lives in the campo. After some time as a sakada in Hawai'i, he moved to California, fell in love with a Mexican girl who was picking lettuce in the neighboring row, and had two daughters.

But it's understood Mang Carlos's proposition isn't serious. Women are rare enough in their community that the mestizas will marry successful men who can bolster the reputation and pockets of their brides' families. Men like Lorenzo, who arrived with almost enough education and almost enough money so that they really do need to work only a few more seasons before they go to college and become lawyers or engineers or doctors. Men whose calluses will soon soften and be forgotten. Men who will make a home of this place.

For the most part, Francisco enjoys working alongside the old-timer, listening to his songs and stories. But whenever he insists on pointing out the white boys going to school, it makes Francisco angry in a subterranean way. It forces him to bury again his quiet resentments.

Francisco's own formal schooling ended after three years, before he could even master reading and writing. He will never be one of those carefree students sauntering to class. His hands are his future. Not his brain. Better to accept that than live a lie and call it hope.

After Mang Carlos, Lorenzo, and Francisco finish laughing at this joke barbed with unintended truth, they fall back into the quiet rhythm of their work.

Cradle, twist, pluck, drop. Cradle, twist, pluck, drop.

Once again Francisco considers asking Mang Carlos about why he insists on pointing out the boys every time they pass, but he doesn't want to disrespect an elder.

"It's good to remember," Mang Carlos offers, since the old man doesn't need to hear a question to know it. "It's good to remember."

But Francisco already understands that if he stays, the best he can hope for is to end up like Mang Carlos: stuck in the fields but at least with a family. More likely his fate would be found with the other old-timers: bachelors with broken backs and faded souls.

"It's good to remember," the old man says again to Francisco or Lorenzo or himself or the leaves.

THE TRAP

"How are you doing, comrade?" asks an unfamiliar and strongly accented voice. The sun is out. It's late morning, the best time of day since it's bright but not yet hot.

"Comrade?" Francisco peeks down through the branches to spot an unfamiliar young man waving at him from the base of his tree with an ungloved hand. Light brown skin. Young face with the shadow of a mustache. The clothes of a laborer but worn like a costume.

Francisco returns to his work. "New here?"

"Yes and no."

"Meaning?"

"New to this orchard, not to the work."

"Of course." Yet he can't be much older than Francisco.

The young man smiles and continues, unprompted. "I've worked the sugarcane plantations in Hawai'i. The canneries in Alaska. The fields up and down this coast."

Francisco says nothing, unimpressed. Who hasn't?

"They always tell you that it is better somewhere else so you'll go there," the young man goes on. "But when you arrive, you realize that even though the scenery has changed, the trap's the same."

"The trap?" Francisco asks, pausing his work to look down again.

"The trap."

"What do you mean?"

He gestures all around.

Francisco understands now. This must be one of those college kids turned organizer. A pensionado from an elite Tagalog family, most likely, who speaks about equality even as his every syllable and mannerism belie a lifetime of privilege. The kind who thinks they can begin a revolution with soft hands and big ideas.

The young man checks over his shoulders as if to make sure nobody's within earshot. Then he removes his cap and stretches out a hand. "I'm Pablo."

Francisco reaches down, and they shake. "Francisco," he says, noting the hand is as soft as expected.

"Nice to meet you, Comrade Isko." The young man named Pablo returns his cap to his head. "May I call you that?"

Francisco nods, though he's not sure if the man's referring to the familiar nickname or that unfamiliar word, *comrade*.

Pablo asks, "You must be . . . what—seventeen, eighteen years old?"

"Sixteen."

Pablo nods as if this is the right answer. "A few of us are going to have a little meeting tonight. You should come."

"Is that so?"

"Yes."

"About what?"

"This trap and how we might free ourselves of it."

Francisco grits his teeth. He's happy to let people live as they want, so long as their choices don't harm others. But even the whisper of a strike could summon the growers' wrath, a wrath that won't distinguish between the workers. He has heard the stories from Mang Carlos and the others, and he has seen it himself a few times.

Francisco turns back to the apples. "No thanks, Mang Pablo. I need that sleep."

"Right, right. I understand. With a face like that, you need all the beauty rest you can get." Pablo smirks.

Francisco cracks a smile and shakes his head but continues plucking apples. His nearly full bag is heavy, the strap digging into his shoulder. "Take care."

But the young man does not leave. "Comrade, did you know you make a fraction of what the white and Mexican laborers make? Do you think that's fair?"

Francisco shrugs, eager for this conversation to end. "There's nothing to be done about it."

"We can all refuse to work until the growers meet our demands."

"The growers will never do that."

"Unless they want their harvest to rot, they'll have no choice."

Francisco shakes his head. "There's no way to get everyone to agree."

"Why not, comrade?" asks Pablo.

"Most us don't even speak the same languages."

"So we learn."

"Even if we could talk to one another," Francisco says, "people look out for themselves first."

"That's what they want us to think."

"Why would they want that?"

"So we never realize our collective power and they can continue to exploit us."

Francisco sighs. "I haven't been here long, but I know if we ask for more, then they'll fire us and find other workers."

"You misunderstand me, little brother. When I say 'all,' I mean 'all.' Not just the Ilokanos, Visayans, and Tagalogs. I mean *all* of the workers. The Filipinos, the Mexicans, the Japanese, the Sikhs, and even the poor whites."

Francisco picks up his pace, plucking and tossing the fruit more aggressively now. "That'll never happen."

"Come to the meeting tonight, and you'll learn more about how it's already happening."

"Right. And since we're dreaming, will you be sending a driver to pick me up? Will there be steak and cigars?"

"You think I'm joking?"

Francisco doesn't bother answering. His sack is full, so he climbs down his ladder. He heads for the large crate at the end of his row and hopes Pablo does not follow.

Pablo follows. "So this is your plan"—the young man holds out his hands, raising his voice—"until you die?"

"Until I can provide a better life for my family," Francisco says.

"What family?" Pablo scoffs. "The whites won't let you marry their daughters, and there are not enough of our women to go around."

Francisco means his family back home; he means he does not intend to stay. But he doesn't share as much because their conversation is drawing the attention of the others. Instead he hefts his sack onto the scale, waits for the weight to be recorded, empties it carefully into the crate, and walks back toward his tree.

"Row after row after row," Pablo continues, punctuating every other word by striking fist to palm and speaking to everyone within earshot. "Day after day after day. Year after year after year. We break our backs sowing and tending and harvesting—yet we reap nothing. Nothing. Remember *that*, comrades. Look at your empty hands each night, each year, and remember *that*."

Mang Carlos and an older Visayan man walk over, grab Pablo roughly by the arms, and lead him away. Francisco climbs back up his ladder.

"You're still young," Pablo calls to Francisco and anyone else still listening. "The trap doesn't need to be your life as it has been for so many of us."

Francisco pretends he cannot hear the young man's parting words as he rustles through the branches in search of the next fruit.

And later that night, Francisco pretends he cannot hear the cries coming from the new tent on the other side of the labor camp as quiet fists and boots and blackjacks crack bones.

And in the dimness of dawn, Francisco pretends he cannot see the body with the soft hands in the ditch as the workers walk past it on their way back to the groves.

THE COSTS

Francisco's drenched in sweat as he wraps up the day, wraps up the job. It's chilly and overcast, but his hat and gloves and boots have been trapping his body heat, making his ill-fitting threadbare clothes cling to his dusty skin.

He empties his final sack into the bin at the end of his row to be picked up by the truck. He removes his hat, wipes the sweat from his brow with the soiled handkerchief tied around his neck, then shoulders his ladder and heads back to camp alongside Lorenzo, Mang Carlos, and the others. His muscles ache and his stomach rumbles since, like most, he did not stop to rest or eat today. It is the last day of the job and, therefore, their last chance to increase their earnings.

❧

That night the workers gather eagerly outside the bunkhouse when the Ilokano contractor arrives with their pay. But Francisco's face falls when the man places the thin pile of cash in his rough palm.

"That's it?" he asks, standing at the cusp of his first off-season.

"That's it," the contractor says.

Francisco moves aside, head hanging, heart heavy. All that work and so little to show for it. Now there are no crops left to harvest and three more months until planting begins. Since he's been unable to save more than a few dollars, he cannot afford to send anything home yet. This disappointing pile must last Francisco through the winter.

He seems alone in his despair as the other men around him count their cash, excited to spend the off-season slipping from city to city, from gambling table to gambling table, from brothel to brothel, bottle to bottle. He and Lorenzo, however, have already decided to stay in Watsonville and try their luck finding jobs in town.

Lorenzo slaps Francisco on the back. "Don't look so glum, little brother. That—plus whatever we make from the work we find—will last."

Lorenzo has the easy faith of someone who's always had enough, and Francisco nods as if he, too, believes. But as they return to their bunks, he cannot help but feel like he is swimming for a boat that's vanishing over the horizon. Maybe Pablo had been right that day in the grove—not about the solution but about the problem.

When Francisco had decided to leave home, he'd been told of farms bursting with produce and not enough hands to harvest. Of endless jobs up and down the coast that paid wages so high, he'd have been a fool not to go. Of the future he could build in a country ripe with opportunity.

They did not tell him of the costs. Clothes, boots, gloves, and hat—all secondhand. A cot. Everything the workers share—the dilapidated cabin or bunkhouse, oil lanterns, oil that lit the lanterns, food, water, tin cups that double as bowls, seeds to plant their own little gardens between their shacks, thread they use to mend their clothes, shovels they use to dig their outhouses and bury their garbage and their dead.

Those costs—along with anything else the growers can quantify—are inflated, then subtracted from their wages at the end of each job. The difference is then handed over to the contractor who arranged the work and who takes a generous cut for doing so before dividing and distributing it to the workers. Some contractors are more generous than others, especially if they are Filipino, and especially if they hail from the same province as their crews. But there is always a chance the contractor will skim more off the top than promised or take all the cash and disappear. How anyone can do that, Francisco does not yet know.

In this way, earnings dissolve bit by bit between the grower's ledger and the contractor's pocket, between the contractor's pocket and the worker's palm, between the worker's palm and the remittance office, between the remittance office and the family's mouths back home.

What remains weighs less than regret.

GHOSTS

Francisco remembers the night his tatang left. He was eight, trying but failing to sleep. As the rain drummed against the nipa roof, he listened to the steady breathing of his younger sister and brothers as they slept next to him. On the other side of the thin walls, their parents argued in hushed voices.

"I'm sorry, Caridad," said his tatang.

"You're always sorry, Francisco," his nanang said to his father, his namesake.

"It will never happen again."

"And you always say that, but it always does."

A carabao lowed in the distance.

His tatang cleared his throat. "She means nothing to me."

"So do I mean even less to you?"

"Please."

"Leave. Now. And don't ever come back."

"What about the kids? They need a father."

"Then tell me when you find a real one for them."

"People will talk."

"Do you think they are not already doing so?"

His tatang's voice shifted then, turned cold and hard. "You can't take care of them on your own."

"What have I been doing for these last three years, ha? As you've been gambling away the last of our pesos and running around with all these women?"

"Without the land—"

"And whose fault is it that we have no more land?"

"They stole it—"

"Ay. Stop it. Nobody 'stole' our land."

"They may as well have. We've become peasants thanks to the Americans' policies. We can't even live off what we produce anymore."

"Stop it, Francisco. Stop blaming others. You are not a victim. They didn't take it. You sold it off piece by piece until there was nothing left."

"To take care of our family!"

"To pay your gambling debts!"

"When there was not enough left, I tried to do what I could to make it enough."

"And how'd that work out?"

Silence.

Francisco's nanang raised her voice. "And you never told me about any of this until there was nothing left. Until it was too late."

"I didn't want to worry you, Caridad. I wanted to figure everything out first."

"We're supposed to figure things out together."

"I am the man of the house! It's my job to—"

"Ay, spare me."

They began shouting over each other, trading insults, not caring if they woke the entire village. Francisco's body tensed as he braced himself for their verbal sparring to turn physical, as it usually did—but instead they suddenly fell quiet. The silence held like the eye of a storm. One of them spat.

"This is no way for a wife to speak to her husband. You keep disrespecting me like this, Caridad, and I really will leave."

"You're the one disrespecting yourself and disrespecting us, Francisco Ramón Reguero Maghabol."

"I'll leave and never come back. I swear to God."

"Go on, then. And if I ever see you again, I will cut off your testicles with the bolo."

"Have it your way. I'm not staying where I'm not wanted."

Footsteps slapped against the muddy ground until they faded away. The rain fell harder. A gust of wind stirred the trees. Francisco's nanang began to sob.

A hand touched his shoulder.

"Manong, are you awake?" his sister, Carmen, whispered. "Did you hear all that?"

Francisco didn't answer his sister. He pretended to be asleep. Pretended not to know.

❦

When the cocks crowed, Francisco slipped out of the hut without waking the others. The pre-dawn air was still cool and the ground damp. Yet the lightening sky was clear enough to see beyond the fields and the trees to the mountains on the eastern horizon, backlit by the rising sun.

Francisco found his tatang's footprints pressed into the mud on the side of their hut. He followed them through the barangay, a few village dogs trailing in his wake, still yawning. If he caught up with his tatang, he did not know if he'd scream at the man or beg him to return. In the end, Francisco didn't have to decide. He lost the trail at the main road amid all the other footprints and tracks, the others who had left or passed by, who'd become ghosts to those they'd loved.

◆

The rest of the family was outside, eating a simple breakfast of bananas and rice, when Francisco returned. His nanang licked her fingers between bites. "Where have you been, boy?"

Francisco shrugged but said nothing. As irrational as it was, he didn't know who deserved his anger the most: his father for his collection of betrayals or his mother for no longer being willing to suffer them.

He made his way to Carmen's side, and she served him a bowl. Their younger brothers quickly devoured their portions and whined for more. There was no more, so Francisco let them split his, and then they ran off to play.

"Where's Tatang?" Francisco asked without looking up, trying to sound casual.

"Not here," his nanang said.

"When will he return?" Carmen asked, trying to sound as casual as Francisco had.

Their nanang did not answer. She would never speak of the man again.

SPACE TO REMEMBER

On Sunday, while men like Mang Carlos attend mass and the less pious head to the farm to bet on pall'ot, Francisco and Lorenzo pile into a jalopy with the others for their weekly trip to Sunset Beach. It's a different kind of religion, much older than Catholicism, this pilgrimage to where land kisses sea like it does in so many places back home.

The sky is overcast and the beach mostly empty given that it's winter. But the salty air is balmy; the wind, calm; the tide, high; and the waves, low. The men accept this as a blessing and waste no time. They roll up their pant legs and remove their boots and socks. Some set off to dig for clams while others grab their poles and brag about how they'll catch so many fish, the jalopy will buckle under the weight of their haul. Cool sand underfoot, they rush to claim the best spots, bait their hooks, and cast their lines like prayers into the waves to catch the perch and jacksmelt that feed in the shallows.

Francisco and Lorenzo take their time. They wander southward down the beach with their poles and buckets, stepping over the clumps of tangled seaweed, shells, and feathers that litter the shore. To their left: the bluffs, carpeted with ice plants and dotted with windswept acacias, eucalyptus, palms. To their right: the gray-blue sea stretching to the horizon, to a homeland both are beginning to fear they may never see again.

When they are far enough away from the others that it feels like they're alone, they wordlessly step into the surf and cast their lines. Then they wait. A couple of boats drift slowly in the distance. A flock of pelicans fly past in formation, the tips of their wings skimming the water's surface. Unbroken clouds slide slowly overhead.

Francisco and Lorenzo say nothing as they fish because nothing needs to be said. In fact, to say something may break the spell of this ritual, which is as sacred as any their ancestors ever practiced. Francisco had learned to fish from his tatang, just as his tatang had learned from his own father, and so on. Even if back home they would more often cast nets instead of lines and work collectively instead of individually, it is the same act of pulling life from the water.

As Francisco's hands wait for the soft tug of a bite, he lets his mind linger on the other side of this ocean. He imagines that a few years have passed and he's made his fortune and returned home. That his little brothers—Juan Luis, José, and Xavier—are splashing in the water, well-fed, well-educated. That his sister, Carmen, is sitting next to him, planning her debut. That their nanang is back home frying freshly slaughtered chicken. That their tatang will return later that night, smelling like the land that is theirs again instead of the woman with the mole on her earlobe.

This weekly trip saves Francisco's soul. It's a pause that gives him space to remember that he's more than a pair of hands in a field. He's more than his labor. He's more than who he is in this country.

It's good to remember, Mang Carlos had said.

Maybe this is what he meant.

ENZO

March 2020
Philadelphia, PA

SNOWFLAKE OBSIDIAN

After school, Enzo and his friend Kyle Sardo check out the New Age shop on Forty-Second. It's a small storefront sandwiched between a board game store and a corner store that sells the city's best bánh mì. Owned by a white woman with dreadlocks, the place is light and airy, filled with boxes of healing crystals, self-help books, tarot card decks, yoga mats, Buddhist prayer flags, incense, and a robust selection of shamanic wands. As Kyle browses, Enzo trails, glued to the news on his phone.

"Shit," Enzo says. "There are so many confirmed cases in Philly right now." He glances around the store as if expecting to see the virus floating in the air.

"No offense, man, but I don't think your obsession with tracking this thing is healthy. You look like you haven't forest bathed in days."

"I have not," Enzo says as he opens a Reddit AMA with someone in an Italian city that's been in lockdown for a couple weeks. "But it's important to stay informed. Look at this chart."

Kyle spins around and snatches Enzo's phone.

"Hey, I was—"

"Consider this an intervention," Kyle says.

Enzo reaches for his phone, but the taller, longer-limbed Kyle holds it out of his reach. Eventually Enzo gives up. "When do I get it back?"

"When you tell me what's got you mad anxious these past few days."

"In case you haven't noticed, we're on the verge of a global pandemic. Doesn't that concern you at all? They're even talking about, like, closing everything down, and—"

"Nothing we can do about it," Kyle interrupts. He's always been chill. A trait that has never rubbed off on Enzo no matter how much time they've spent together. "But I've known you long enough to know there's something else going on."

Enzo wanders away, feigning sudden interest in the bonsai trees on the other side of the store as Kyle follows. He doesn't want to sound like the whiny, privileged American he probably is. But then he remembers Dr. Mendoza always saying how men often feel overwhelmingly lonely because they don't know how talk to one another, and he turns to face his friend.

"It's my lolo," Enzo admits.

"Ah, there it is. What's going on exactly?"

"I don't know, man." Enzo pauses, searching for the right words to describe what it's been like to live with the man.

Lolo Emil's presence is old-people smell. It is pill bottles crowding the bathroom sink and prune juice colonizing the fridge. It is the shuffle of house slippers, the grinding of coffee beans too early in the morning. It is constant coughing and throat clearing. It is the only bathroom occupied for longer than seems humanly necessary. It is Thor's putrid farts and constant shedding. It is the TV blasting golf or reality shows about hoarders or the local news at nearly max volume. It is Enzo and Chris pausing their rewatch of *Avatar: The Last Airbender*. It is the thermostat mysteriously turned down ten degrees. It is *Why do you always have to cook something ethnic?* and then adding salt to the meal before tasting it. It is *Your hair makes you look like a girl* and *Stand up straight* and *Does anyone in this house know how to turn off the lights when they're not in a room?*

It is the family's collective exhale when Lolo Emil takes Thor on his long morning and evening walks. It is Julia staying late at the university or keeping her office door shut when she works from home. It is Chris smoking for the first time in nearly ten years. It is Enzo in exile, sleeping on the living room couch instead of in his room.

And Enzo's room is not just a room. It's more than a space to sleep or study in. It's more than storage for his stuff. At Dr. Mendoza's suggestion, he'd put a lot of thought and time over the years into intentionally arranging the space until it felt as though it restored his soul—like the chair by his window with the bamboo palm where he used to sit and listen to music as he journaled or read.

"He's been living with us for a couple weeks," Enzo says, "and I thought it'd be easier by now."

"What's been hard about it?"

Enzo tries describing as best he can what it's been like living with Lolo Emil, not having his room anymore, how the old man's presence has him feeling like a planet knocked off its orbit.

"Yeah," Kyle says when Enzo finishes talking, "that sounds rough, man."

"I'm not overreacting?"

"No, dude," Kyle says. "It's like when my cousins from Japan stayed with my family last summer and I had to share my room."

Enzo laughs, remembering. "You were so sick of them, you tried to rent that place down the street."

"And I would've succeeded if Airbnb didn't require users to be eighteen. Point is, it's hard to share your space like that."

Enzo holds his problem up in the light against those of others. Children who spend their days working in mines so the rest of the world can have smartphones. People suffering from starvation, disease, political persecution. Refugees who have been forced to flee their homes and have lost everything, everyone, because of their corrupt governments' wars or because of natural disasters exacerbated by climate change thanks to exploitative corporations. People dying from this new virus that's spreading faster and faster across the world every day.

"But people are dying," he says.

"People are always dying," Kyle says.

"Yeah, but—"

"After you read that one book your therapist recommended, you told me to call you out whenever you started to minimize your feelings."

"I'm not doing that now."

"You're doing that now, dude. You don't need to compare what you're going through with every single other terrible thing going on in the world. Those things can be happening *and* you can be struggling with stuff in your own life."

Enzo sighs. His friend has a point. "Thanks, man."

"I got you. You got me. That's how this friendship thing works."

"So what should I do?" Enzo asks. "Airbnb?"

Kyle makes his way back over to the bins of stones and crystals. He plucks one out of a pile and holds it up to examine it in the sunlight spilling through the storefront windows. It's opaque black speckled with white. Satisfied, he turns and hands it to Enzo. "Snowflake obsidian. It'll keep you centered in chaotic situations."

Enzo turns it over in his palm, closes his eyes, and takes a deep breath. "Ah yes. I feel it centering me already."

"You do?"

Enzo opens one eye. "If I say yes, will you give me back my phone?"

Kyle sucks his teeth and snatches the stone from Enzo. He takes it to the register, pays, and hands it back to Enzo. "Keep the stone on the windowsill by that chair of yours."

"I don't have that windowsill anymore," Enzo reminds him.

"Then keep it in your pocket." They step out of the store and into the early spring afternoon, and Kyle passes Enzo back his phone. "Want to hit up the rec next?"

Enzo thinks of the poorly ventilated indoor basketball courts. The skin-to-skin contact, the heavy breathing, the sweating. And he thinks about a video he saw recently. A hospital in Italy that was so overcrowded, the hallways were lined with beds. It must have been the middle of the night because the lights were low and it was quiet except for the strained wheezing of patients fighting through ventilators for each breath not to be their last.

"Think I'm going to pass today," he says.

"You sure?" Kyle asks.

"I'm sure," Enzo says.

"Up to you. I'm gonna try to run a game or two, though."

"Think that's a good idea?" Enzo asks.

"What? Because of this virus?"

"Yeah."

Kyle shrugs. "The number of cases in Philly sounds like a lot, but remember how many people live in this city. Statistically, I'll probably be fine."

"'Probably' doesn't mean 'definitely.'"

"Nothing is definite."

With that, Kyle moves to hug Enzo goodbye, but Enzo holds out his fist for a bump instead. Kyle bumps it without saying anything, without making Enzo feel like he's being overly cautious.

This, however, will be the last time they touch for months.

ADULTS

The next day, the city declares extensive community quarantine measures, and the school district announces the cancellation of in-person classes. That evening Enzo's dad is sitting on the top step of their stoop, smoking as he watches the empty street. A book about the Philippine village at the 1904 St. Louis World's Fair lies closed on one side of him, a half-empty bottle of beer on the other.

"Can we talk?" Enzo asks.

Chris takes a drag of his cigarette, lost in thought. "Now's not a great time, anak."

The dismissal stings. Enzo starts to leave but then decides he needs to not be turned away, even if he knows he shouldn't cross a clear boundary his dad has set. It's great that his dad supports Enzo's therapy, but it doesn't let Chris off the hook when it comes to having real conversations with his son.

"It's about Lolo Emil," Enzo starts as he sits down.

His dad raises his eyebrow, a reluctant invitation to continue with caution.

"How much longer do you think he'll be staying with us?" There's a new urgency to the question now that it looks like they're all going to be stuck at home for the foreseeable future.

"I suppose until it's safe out there."

"And how long will that take?"

Chris shrugs. "That's the million-dollar question, isn't it?"

A car passes, bass thumping.

When the music fades, Enzo asks, "What if we found him his own place?"

Chris takes a drink. "We can't afford that."

"Are you certain? I'm sure he'd be happier," Enzo adds.

"He'd be happier, or you'd be happier?" Chris asks. There's an edge to his voice, the old anger that rears its head when he's stressed.

"Both?" Enzo offers. "I mean, hasn't it been difficult for you having him here all the time?"

Chris takes another drink. Then another. "I know you're not used to sharing your space since you're an only child, Enzo. And I know you've grown up with this selfish Western attitude that teaches that the elderly are nothing but an inconvenience. But in the East, they're respected. They're family. They're the reason we're here. We honor them, and when they need us, we take care of them. We talked about this already: utang na loob."

"Even if they're completely toxic?"

"Everything's 'toxic' to your generation."

Enzo flushes with a mixture of shame and annoyance. Chris had also been born and raised in America, so didn't he share those attitudes, no matter how much he self-educated later in life? When Lolo Emil had first raised the idea of moving into a retirement home after Grandma Linda passed, Chris hadn't objected.

The streetlamps flicker on, though it's still light out.

Chris continues, voice softening. "Think about it this way: Your lolo is mostly healthy right now, but he's old. He's not going to be around forever. You haven't spent too much time around him. Only a couple of hours every few months—and that's my fault. Consider this a good opportunity to get to know him. To let him get to know you."

His dad isn't listening. The problem isn't that he doesn't know Lolo Emil well enough. It's that he's invaded their space and has already started fucking up their family dynamics. It's that this can only get worse now that they're all going to be trapped together.

"What about you?" Enzo asks.

"What about me?"

"You've been doing everything you can to avoid him, and he's *your* father."

Chris looks at Enzo, annoyed to be called out by his own child.

"And not just since he's moved in," Enzo adds.

Chris takes one last drag, then snuffs out the cigarette, dropping the butt in an old University of Colorado mug he's started keeping out on the porch, not ready to commit to an actual ashtray again. He takes a deep breath but doesn't say anything for a while. And then: "You should join him on his evening walks."

"Are you serious?" Enzo says.

"I am. That's the perfect opportunity to get to know him. Plus, isn't it supposed to be good for your mental health to exercise?"

"Will you be joining us?"

Enzo dad's laughs, pats Enzo on the shoulder, and heads back inside.

Adults. Nothing if not reliable in their hypocrisy.

THIS IS FINE

As Dr. Young predicted, the virus spreads rapidly, hitting hardest in nursing homes, retirement communities, prisons, and anywhere else large groups of people are trapped together in close quarters. Hospitals are overwhelmed, and healthcare workers lack basic protective gear. More and more videos circulate online of people in ICU beds wheezing, of doctors and nurses pleading for help. Morgues run out of space and rent refrigerated trailers to hold the extra bodies.

People complain about the closing of movie theaters, bars, gyms, museums, parks, and other businesses deemed "nonessential." School remains virtual. Concerts, conventions, sports, and other events are cancelled. Restaurants shift to delivery or takeout only. Pretty much the only public spots open in Philly are grocery stores and hospitals.

With basically nowhere to go in the real world, Enzo's life becomes almost entirely virtual. He completes his digital school assignments. He plays online games with Kyle. He hops on Discord with some of their other friends to group-watch shows or movies online. He starts meeting with his therapist on a video chat app in Julia's office, paranoid his family can hear him through the walls.

And, of course, he doomscrolls:

Charts with steeply rising lines.

Proper handwashing instructions.

People hoarding toilet paper and hand sanitizer.

Debates about the minor inconvenience of wearing a mask.

Workers whose pay and treatment suggest they are less essential than proclaimed.

Nurses and doctors receiving applause but little else.

Disabled people and the elderly discussed as disposable.

Personal story after personal story of those who've lost loved ones to the virus, pleading for society to take this seriously.

Still, Enzo completes the minimal work assigned by his school. He eats. He shows up to his virtual obligations, smiles, and says, *Bored*, when anyone asks how he's doing. He doesn't complain, because who is he to complain? At the moment, he's safe. The people immediately around him are safe. He has food and water, a place to live, reliable internet access. His parents have jobs that allow them to work from home.

Yet, on the inside, the buzzing in Enzo's mind has become relentless, the murder hornets swarming. They're louder than his music. Louder than the wind rustling the leaves. Louder than deep breathing or journaling or video games or TV or books or the sounds of his therapist's or parents' or friends' voices. His chest feels tight. His stomach constantly churns with nausea. There's no space for anything in his mind other than worry. Basically, he's feeling all the physical sensations of anxiety he's been taught to notice so that he can acknowledge them and remind himself that they will pass. Only they are not passing.

Chris and Julia have always emphasized the importance of paying attention to what's happening in the world, about the moral responsibility to help those in need and to change unjust systems however and wherever one can. But there's too much going on. Too much Enzo can do absolutely nothing about.

"Have you been thinking about hurting yourself?" Dr. Mendoza asks onscreen after Enzo finally decides to share all of this.

"No," Enzo says truthfully. "It's not that. I just don't want to feel like this all the time."

Dr. Mendoza starts to say something, but the connection glitches.

"What?" Enzo asks. "You froze again."

"I said, have you given any more consideration to medication or spoken to your parents about the possibility?"

Enzo shrugs, looks away from the screen. "Maybe I'd be okay if my lolo never moved in with us," he says, dodging the question.

"Go on."

Enzo idly moves the cursor around his screen. "It's stupid to even think that. It's, like, I don't know. Why would I wish he remained in some place where he might catch the virus and die just so I don't have to deal with him? I guess I'm a horrible person?"

Dr. Mendoza talks for a while, but Enzo misses most of it because the connection keeps cutting out.

"I'll be okay," Enzo says when it's his turn to speak. "It's really not as serious as all that. I just need to be like the cartoon dog in that one meme that's sipping coffee in a house on fire. You know, 'This is fine.'"

"You do understand the whole point of that meme is that the dog is definitely not fine?"

"He looks like he's doing all right to me."

"If the dog continues to pretend like nothing's happening around him, he will burn alive."

"Is there any other way to survive in the middle of a disaster?"

"Yeah," Dr. Mendoza says. "There is."

SOME COMPANY

After dinner one night, Lolo Emil goes to the door and slips on his jacket. Thor does that little tippy-tappy dance he does when it's time to walk, nails clicking against the hardwood floor. Chris catches Enzo's eye and points with his lips toward Lolo Emil.

Enzo sighs, turns to the old man. "Hey, Lolo, want some company on your walk?"

Lolo Emil clips on Thor's leash. "No."

"Dad—" Chris starts to say, but the door slams shut before he can finish.

"I tried," Enzo says.

Chris stares at the closed door, jaw clenched, eerily still. Julia puts a hand on his forearm as if to keep him grounded.

"It's okay, Dad," Enzo says.

Chris pushes away from the table, grabs his pack of cigarettes and lighter from the counter, and disappears through the back door.

CHRIS

November 1983
Denver, CO

WAITING TO BE DISCOVERED

Chris sits at a table on the upper floor of the public library, near the western-facing windows. Horror comic in hand, he gazes out at the overcast sky and the slices of the Front Range peeking between the city's gray buildings. School only let out half an hour ago, but the world is already dimming as the November sun sinks.

It's been two weeks since Emil ruined Chris's life and barred him from the football team. Now, instead of going to practice after school, he's condemned to the library each day until 5:30 p.m., when Emil can pick him up on his way home from the office. Chris is supposed to use his daily sentence to complete his homework. Out of protest, he does nothing. He is a pilot nose-diving his plane into the sea with no plan to pull up this time.

All because of that history assignment. Students were supposed to research a topic of their choice related to their "ancestral history." Chris didn't know anything about his "ancestral history," so he'd procrastinated until he'd forgotten about it. Though Ms. Pérez agreed to accept the assignment late for partial credit, Emil had not changed his mind. Chris had slipped up. He must face the consequences. How else would he learn?

"You're Hazel Young's friend, right?" someone says, drawing Chris's eyes away from the window. It's the new girl. The one from the Philippines. "Chris?"

"Yeah, that's me." Chris sits up, intrigued. He's seen her around school, and Hazel has a couple of classes with her. But this is the first time they've spoken to each other despite everyone else's expectation that they'd hit it off simply because they were Filipino.

"Becs," she says, smiling. "Short for Rebecca Sales."

"Oh. Cool. Chris is short for . . . Christopher. Maghabol."

"Interesting surname," she says—but not with the usual tone his white classmates and teachers use when they call it that. " 'To chase' in Tagalog or 'to weave' in Bikol, right?"

"Yup," Chris says, even though he doesn't know either of those languages or any translation of his last name.

"Which is your family: Tagalog or Bikolano?"

Another simple question Chris can't answer truthfully. This time, though, he doesn't pretend. "I'm not actually sure."

"Oh." Becs pauses as if considering what to say next. "Anyway, mind if I sit with you?"

"Go for it." He gestures to the seat across from him even if he doesn't know why she wants to when there are plenty of other open tables.

Whatever the reason, Becs sets a stack of books on the table and sits. She spots Chris's horror comic and raises her eyebrow. "Hard at work, ha?"

Chris quickly closes the comic. It's a weird one. "Just warming up."

"Ah, I see. So, what are you working on today?"

He shrugs. "Nothing, really."

Becs brushes a strand of straight black hair behind an ear and gives him a confused smile. "Nothing?"

"Nope."

"Then why are you here?"

Chris considers giving some vague response, but since Becs genuinely seems interested, he tries to explain the situation with his dad. Even as he's talking, he's aware of how petty and immature he sounds—Hazel has already told him as much. Sure enough, when he finishes, Becs's confused smile is still fixed in place.

"So," she says, "you're mad at your father, and you're getting back at him by . . . wasting your own time and ruining your own life?"

"Well, no. Not exactly. It's more like . . ." Chris pauses, searching for a better explanation. "I'm trying to show him he can't control me."

Becs lifts an eyebrow again. "By ruining your own life?"

"I'm not ruining my life."

"Okay."

"But if that's what it takes, then, yeah. Sure."

The conversation stalls—an awkward moment given how quickly this person he's only just met has peered into the core of his being. Nonetheless, Becs cracks open one of her textbooks and a notebook, pulls out a pen, and gets to work as if that's not what she has done.

Chris starts to reach for his comic but then glances at Becs and grabs his history folder instead. Reluctantly, he takes out the directions page for the ancestral history paper he still hasn't completed and places it on the table. After rereading the instructions yet again, he lets out a heavy groan.

"What's wrong?" Becs asks, looking up.

"This stupid assignment," he says. He starts spinning the paper on the table.

Becs snatches it and reads the directions aloud. "Sounds interesting," she declares when she gets to the end. "They never gave assignments like this back in the Philippines."

He shrugs. "I have no idea what topic to pick. Hazel did hers on Black cowboys in the Old West because apparently her great-grandfather or something was one. But, like, my family has no 'ancestral history.'"

"Everyone's from somewhere."

"My mom's from Colorado, and my dad—"

"He's from the Philippines, like me?"

"His parents were," Chris corrects. "He was born in California. But he never talks about his family. Doesn't even have a single picture from his childhood. It's like he popped out of the womb with a mustache and slide rule."

"See."

"What?"

"Both sides of your family are from somewhere."

"Yeah, but one side's from here—which is pretty boring—and the other side's from somewhere I don't know anything about."

"Having roots in the place where you currently live isn't boring," she says. "It's a privilege. As for your dad's side . . ." She furrows her brow in deep thought. "If only you could find a building filled with vast amounts of information on a whole range of topics."

Chris widens his eyes. "Wow, such magical places exist?"

Becs laughs as she hands back his directions page.

"Speaking of families," Chris says as he puts it away, "why'd yours move here?"

Becs's expression darkens. She picks up her pen and begins scribbling on the lined paper. She's quiet for a long time before simply saying, "Marcos."

"Who's that?"

She looks up. "Ferdinand Marcos?"

Chris waits for her to explain who that is and what he has to do with her family moving to the United States.

"The Philippine dictator who's been in power for almost twenty years?"

Chris fidgets. "Sorry, I've never heard of him."

Her eyes dim with disappointment. She shakes her head and mutters to herself, "Fil-Ams . . ." followed by something in a language Chris assumes is Filipino.

"I told you I didn't know anything about the Philippines."

"I didn't realize you were being literal."

The comment stings. Chris lets a few beats of silence pass, then tries to move in a different direction. "This Marcos guy—you said he's, like, a dictator or something?"

Becs sighs as she turns to a fresh page in her notebook. "Yeah. But I've got this essay to write, so . . . do you mind?"

"Oh. Right. Sure. Sorry."

Becs throws Chris a small smile, then puts pen to paper and disappears. Chris goes back to reading his comic.

❧

An hour later, Becs checks her watch, caps her pen, and closes her notebook. "I have to get home," she says, "but thanks for letting me sit with you."

"No problem," Chris says. "Guess I'll see you around school."

She offers him one last smile and walks away, disappearing into the stacks. Chris turns back to the window. The sun has set. The streetlights are lit. There's no snow, but the city seems cold as hell.

After Chris is certain Becs is gone, he heads over to the reference section and grabs the *P* volume of the encyclopedia. He used to read random entries from his family's set at home for fun when he was little. Why had he stopped? School, probably.

He flips to the entry on the Philippines. It's much longer than he expected. Since they never learned about the country in any of his classes, he had assumed it wasn't that important, relatively speaking.

As he skims the first few sections—geography, agriculture, natural resources, and such—the flood of unfamiliar facts overwhelms him. He calls this feeling *museum head* because it reminds him of when Emil drags the family to a museum. In the moment, Chris feels like he's learning so much as he looks at the artifacts and reads the placards. But there always comes a point—usually after an hour or so—when his brain feels full, and he'll wander through the rest of the museum mentally numb, pretending to read everything. Then, when they leave, Emil will quiz him and his sisters on the info from the exhibits, and Chris will hardly remember anything.

When he reaches the history section of the entry, Chris slows down. Maybe he'll finally find a topic for his paper.

The Philippine Islands were discovered by Ferdinand Magellan in March 1521, reads the first sentence.

He pauses.

Did he miss something? Why does it begin there?

There are a few accounts of the early Spanish explorers' encounters with "the natives" in different parts of the country, which kind of answers one of his questions. But if this is supposed to be about the history of the Philippines, why does it read like the history of Spain? What about all those centuries before 1521? Were the people just hanging out, waiting to be discovered, waiting to exist?

The entry goes on to describe the development of major Spanish colonies. There are a few mentions of "discontent" and failed rebellions, which pique Chris's interest. It'd be cool to learn more about those, but there are only brief references. Even the section on José Rizal—apparently one of the leaders of the revolution, and the first named Filipino the entry describes after summarizing about three hundred years—only takes up a short paragraph. Then it talks about the Philippine-American War—which Chris has never learned about in school—and the ensuing years of American colonialism up through World War II.

Toward the end of the history section, Chris learns that Ferdinand Marcos is a lawyer turned politician who was elected president in 1965. But there's not much more information beyond that. Nothing about him being a dictator. Nothing to suggest why he might have caused Becs's family to leave.

Chris checks the copyright page and finds that this edition came out just a few years after that election. He considers searching for an updated version, but it's almost time for Emil to pick him up.

He rubs his eyes and shuts the heavy book, frustrated and ashamed by how much he doesn't know about his ancestors, angry at Emil and the American school system for never teaching him.

That's not your country, Emil would say whenever Chris or his sisters asked about the Philippines. *You're American.*

"Do you have any questions, young man?" a passing librarian asks as Chris slides the volume back into place on the shelf.

"Too many," Chris says.

The librarian laughs. "Then you're in the right place."

THE NEW SOCIETY

Chris's forced library time transforms from his punishment to his purpose: researching Ferdinand Marcos, the topic he's finally selected for his very overdue project. He endures the school day, aching for the stacks like he used to ache for the football field, then rushes over as soon as the dismissal bell rings. He loses himself in the card catalogue and Dewey Decimal System and dusty books nobody's checked out in years. He learns how to use microfilm and microfiche. He befriends the reference librarians, who supply him with endless recommendations and teach him to skim, to note, to cite. Sometimes Hazel joins him to work on her own assignments and to remind him that he has other classes and other work to do, but most days he goes alone. It never feels like he has enough time, and each day, Chris struggles to peel himself away from whatever he's reading as the clock nears five thirty.

From the encyclopedias, Chris learns the basics about Ferdinand Marcos, like how he was from a northern province called Ilocos Norte on the island of Luzon and how his father was a prominent politician. He learns about how Marcos was a brilliant lawyer who rose through the ranks of the Philippine political system. How he married a beautiful woman named Imelda, who was from the poorer side of a powerful political family and whose personality and charm boosted his public image exponentially. How he was elected to the presidency in 1965 and reelected in

1969—making him the only person to serve twice as Philippine president. How he declared martial law in 1972 and is still in power eleven years later.

And then, with the help of one of the research librarians, Dr. Bishop, Chris digs deeper. They find a 1940 article about how the man was found guilty of murdering his father's political rival and sentenced to death—only for the Supreme Court to overturn that decision.

"Did you know that?" Chris asks his dad after sharing this info in the car on the way home that day, astounded that someone could ascend from assassin to president.

"Hmm," Emil says.

"And," Chris goes on, "I read somewhere else that Marcos claims that he was the most decorated Filipino soldier during World War II, but he's been lying about that apparently. Like, just saying he won all these awards when he didn't. And he was captured by the Japanese at one point, but then he was released because his dad was actually helping the Japanese, which is messed up, right? Oh, but Filipino guerillas eventually killed his dad because of that."

"Christopher," Emil says, "I'm trying to drive."

One Friday, Dr. Bishop hands Chris a book titled *The Conjugal Dictatorship of Ferdinand and Imelda Marcos*. "It's a tell-all by this man named Primitivo Mijares, who was Ferdinand Marcos's chief propagandist. He defected, testified in the US against Marcos, and published this book."

"Wow," Chris says. "Can't imagine Marcos took that well?"

"No, he did not," Dr. Bishop says. "Mr. Mijares disappeared shortly after the book's publication in 1977, on his way back to his family in the

Philippines. And a few months after that, his fifteen-year-old son was tortured and stabbed to death."

Chris looks down at the book in his hands, appreciating for the very first time in his life the danger and power of words on paper.

He spends the weekend devouring those words. He learns how, as the end of his second term neared, Marcos played up the threat of Communist rebel groups to justify his declaration of martial law in 1972 so that he wouldn't have to give up power, going so far as to stage attempted assassinations of government officials that he could place the blame for on the Communists. How he immediately shut down the free press, began arresting potential political opponents, restricted travel outside of the country, confiscated weapons from private citizens, instituted a strict curfew, shut down all schools for a week, banned public protests, and made it illegal for anyone to question the legality of his actions in the courts.

Chris learns how Marcos places friends and family and in-laws in powerful government positions, like how he appointed Imelda as the governor of the Greater Manila Region and her brother as ambassador to the US. How he grants himself lucrative contracts, monopoly deals, and tax exemptions. How he pockets some of the money Japan pays to the Philippines as reparations for WWII. How he uses his power and influence to shift ownership of the most profitable businesses and industries in the names of his friends, who then transfer a majority ownership to an unnamed individual everyone knows is Marcos himself.

During dinner one night, Chris sits at the table with another book open beside his plate. Without taking his eyes off the page, he tells his family: "Did you know that nearly half the population in the Philippines lives on about two dollars per day, but the Marcoses own multiple homes all over the world, a five-million-dollar yacht, helicopters, and dozens of Mercedes-Benzes?"

"Nobody cares," Amy says, then takes a bite of pot roast.

Chris goes on, paraphrasing the open page. "Imelda has thousands of pairs of designer shoes, buys the most expensive perfumes by the gallon, takes a bunch of overseas trips with entourages of up to, like, eighty people, owns multiple paintings by the most famous artists, and even tried to buy Tiffany & Co."

"Christopher," Emil says sternly. "We're at the table. Put the book away."

"Sure, Dad, but I just want to finish this ch—"

Emil reaches across the table and slams it shut.

Chris stops reading at the table, but he does not stop reading. From first- and secondhand accounts, Chris learns how thousands of activists and political opponents have been imprisoned and tortured. How there is something called the San Juanico Bridge, where guards force prisoners to lie naked across two beds and then beat them when their suspended body sags. How they drug and rape and shock with electricity. How they beat pregnant prisoners until they miscarry. How they press hot irons across the soles of feet and put out cigarettes on eyelids and mouths and genitals. How mutilated bodies have been found in mass graves, and how hundreds of others have simply disappeared after being taken from their homes. How Muslim Filipinos in the south have been massacred for resisting Marcos's rule.

And from the research of a Filipino American professor at Temple University in Philadelphia, Chris learns how, despite Marcos's initial claim that martial law would grant him the freedom to enact reforms that would build "the New Society" and make their country great again, inflation and the national debt are skyrocketing while the wages of farmers and unskilled and skilled workers are plummeting. In the meantime, Marcos's family has been stealing the equivalent of billions of dollars that should be used to improve the country for the people.

The more Chris learns, the better he understands why Becs thought she only needed to say the dictator's name to explain why her family moved out of the country. He wonders about the exact shape of their suffering. But whenever Chris passes Becs at school, he avoids making eye contact, bowed by the shame of all he did not know, all he still does not know, all he will never truly know due to the privilege of distance.

I May Not Be Able to Talk to You Again After This

The week before Thanksgiving, Chris is in his favorite study room finally drafting his paper when there's a knock on the door. He opens it to find Dr. Bishop pushing a cart with a TV and VCR.

"Tracked down something else you might want to see," she says.

Chris steps out of the way so she can wheel it into the small windowless room. "Thanks. What is it?"

"A news report. From a couple of months back."

"About Marcos?"

"You'll see." She plugs in the TV and VCR, then turns them on. "I'll leave you to it," she says before heading out.

Excited to see what's on the tape, Chris turns off the lights, hits play, and sits down. A white news anchor with brown hair, an oval face, and sympathetic eyes sits at a desk, a sheaf of papers in hand. He rattles off a preview of the evening's top stories in that practiced news anchor voice.

Then the camera switches, and the anchor shifts in his seat to directly face the audience. The image of a friendly-looking Filipino guy with big glasses appears in a box over the reporter's shoulder. Thanks to all his research, Chris recognizes him immediately.

Benigno Aquino was regarded in the Philippines as the strongest challenger to the rule of President Ferdinand Marcos. Today, after three years of self-exile, Aquino returned to the Philippines to try to restore democracy there, ignoring threats against his life. Within minutes, he was assassinated.

Chris leans forward, stunned. Aquino was assassinated? He hadn't come across that yet in any of the research he'd done. Dr. Bishop had said this was from a couple of months ago—so maybe August or September?

The anchor goes on. *The Marcos government said the killer slipped through security wearing the uniform of an airport worker. But some eyewitnesses said that Philippine soldiers shot Aquino. We have two reports tonight on the murder of the man in the Philippines known as "Ninoy."*

The screen cuts to a video of Aquino sitting on an airplane dressed in white pants and a white short-sleeved button-up shirt. As the other passengers board, he smiles and chats and laughs and shakes hands as if they're all good friends.

Chris scoots his chair closer.

Upon arriving in Manila, three stone-faced Filipino soldiers board the plane. Aquino shakes their hands, as if they, too, were old friends. Then the soldiers escort him off the plane, through the gangway, and to the exit that leads to the runway.

The camera tries to follow, but soldiers block everyone's way. Things grow frantic as people try to push past. Unconsciously, Chris half rises out of his chair, as if changing his angle might improve the view. The camera points higher to try to capture what's happening outside, but the light washes out the image over the crowd's heads. Then—

POP! A gunshot rings out, making Chris jump.

There are exclamations and cries and chaos as people jostle unsuccessfully toward the exit.

Several more gunshots.

And then several more—louder, closer to the camera, impossible to count.

Chris is on his feet, heart pounding. The video cuts to a shaky, grainy zoomed-in shot of two bodies lying on the tarmac, unmoving—one dressed in white. The voice-over of a male reporter identifies the bodies as Aquino and the alleged assassin, supposedly killed by the soldiers. Then there's a van driving away with Aquino. Then back to the other man's body, which the reporter says was left on the tarmac for four hours.

As the camera cuts to a crowd of onlookers, the reporter informs the viewers, *Some eyewitnesses said the soldiers shot Aquino, then led the man they described as the assassin to the spot and shot him. But government doctors who examined the body said Aquino had been shot once in the head, supporting the soldiers' account of his death.*

Of course the government doctors would say that, Chris thinks. Perhaps once an assassin, always an assassin—giving orders instead of pulling triggers now.

Chris stops the tape. Takes a moment to catch his breath, to let his heart rate slow. Then he rewinds and rewatches to make sure it was real. Then he rewinds and rewatches a second time, paying closer attention to everything happening in the background of every frame.

Finally he sits back down and lets the recording advance past the assassination. The video shows the crowd who had come to the airport with signs and smiles to welcome Aquino home while the reporter explains that Aquino had been aware of threats on his life and had discussed that the previous evening.

Then Aquino's on the screen—not an unmoving body on a tarmac, but alive in the interview from the previous night. Aquino advises the interviewer to be ready to film his arrival because the assassination might happen very quickly. He looks down, laughs nervously, then raises his eyes to meet the interviewer's.

I may not be able to talk to you again after this, he says with a sad, knowing smile.

After a few more words from Aquino about how he'll wear a bullet-proof vest and might be okay so long as they don't shoot him in the head, the segment concludes and transitions to the reactions to the assassination in Manila.

There's a forlorn-looking group surrounding a weeping woman. A crowd of protestors with yellow headbands shouting and holding fists and signs in the air. A man with a megaphone demanding justice and asking the crowd to pray for Aquino. A row of women kneeling in a church pew with shirts that read *Ninoy pa rin kami*. More shaky, grainy clips from the tarmac in the moments after the assassination that don't really show anything.

Then it's back to the studio and the brown-haired, oval-faced white anchor with the soft eyes. He talks about how Aquino's family had been living in exile in the United States but now planned to return to Manila for the funeral. A woman identified as Corazon Aquino, Ninoy's widow, explains that he had expected this as a risk of holding public office, but that she didn't believe it would actually happen.

The reporter shares a statement from Ferdinand Marcos about how they had warned Aquino that "certain elements" would try to kill him if he should return, but that what had happened was a "heinous" crime. Then he describes President Reagan's close relationship with Marcos and his condemnation of the murder.

The camera cuts to a Black reporter standing in front of a palm tree who states that President Reagan intends to travel to the Philippines in November as part of a previously planned trip to different parts of Asia, making Chris wonder if he is there at this very moment. The reporter goes on to explain how the dictator has been in power for eighteen years after being elected president, declaring martial law, and instituting "constitutional authoritarianism"; how there were numerous charges of human rights abuses against him; and how the US and President Reagan supported him anyway because the islands are key to US military and economic strategy in the Pacific.

The Black reporter signs off, and the white one in the studio transitions to the next story—something about a telephone company strike. But then there's a jolt of static snow across the screen, and the news report is replaced by an episode of *Dallas* that must have been taped over.

Chris lets it play as he sits in stunned silence. A disoriented, unsettling feeling swirls in his stomach. An end-of-the-ride feeling, like when the roller coaster clanks back to the platform, the crossbar rises, and the riders shamble away with shaky legs and stuttering souls.

Chris climbs into his dad's car practically vibrating with belated outrage at the injustice of Aquino's assassination. Why didn't he hear anything about it before now? Hell, why didn't he know anything about Marcos before Becs? Maybe his ignorance is his fault. But maybe not entirely. You don't know what you don't know, and how many people had to have failed so that there was so much Chris didn't know?

"Did you hear about what happened to Ninoy?" he asks Emil immediately after he pulls the passenger door closed.

Emil checks his rearview mirror. Signals. Pulls away from the library. "Who?"

"Benigno Aquino."

Emil thinks for a moment. "That politician assassinated in the Philippines a little while back?"

"Yes," Chris says. "And?"

"And what?"

"And what do you think about it?"

Emil shrugs. "Third-world countries are an absolute mess, so I'm grateful we live in America."

Chris turns to Emil, unable to mask his disgust. "You don't care at all about what's happening over there?"

"No," Emil says, his face lit by the red glow of a stoplight. "And neither should you."

Chris starts to argue, but his dad cuts him a familiar stony look.

"Careful," Emil cautions, like smothering a fire.

Is there any argument that will get through to his dad? Unable to find the words that might make the fight worth the energy, Chris bites his tongue yet again. He crosses his arms and turns to face the window, extinguished.

EMIL

August 1965
Stockton, CA

How We Fight

Francisco comes and goes throughout the summer, recruiting Filipinos across the state to join the strike that's to begin in early September at the cusp of the grape harvest. As August wanes and Francisco prepares to leave for Delano once more, Emil finds himself up early and walking with Francisco into the boxing gym with the high ceilings that used to be a dance hall. The place is dimly lit and stinks of old sweat. A pair of men spars in the ring at the center. A few hit the heavy bags or the speed bags. Others skip rope or lift weights. The sounds of shuffling feet, panting lungs, and thwacking gloves fill the air.

Nothing's changed, and there's something sad about that to Emil. They used to come here every Sunday morning whenever Francisco was in town. But when Francisco's absences became more frequent as Emil got older, Emil stopped reaching for his gloves and instead began grabbing his fishing pole and heading to the river on Sunday mornings to spend a few hours alone with the water, the trees, and the sky. But today, Francisco insisted the two of them head back to this dank, dreary place.

Emil waits as Francisco greets every single person in the gym, and then they make their way to one of the narrow wooden benches that line the walls. They sit, and Francisco begins taping his own wrists. "I'm glad we're getting to spend some time together," he says in English, voice hoarse from all the speeches he's been giving while in town.

Emil crosses his arms and leans back. "Before you leave again, you mean."

"It's good to be back here with you, is all."

Emil says nothing. Francisco rips a strip of tape with his teeth, finishes wrapping his hands, then holds out the roll to Emil.

"No thanks."

Francisco raises an eyebrow. "For old times' sake, ha?"

Emil shakes his head.

Francisco sighs, sets down the tape, and slips on his gloves. He holds them out to Emil to tie, and Emil ties them. "Make yourself useful, then, and hold the bag for me."

Emil gets up and follows his father to a punching bag. He moves behind it, setting his feet and positioning his shoulder against the cracking leather, readying himself to absorb the hits.

After rolling out his neck and bouncing on the balls of his feet a few times, Francisco starts warming up with slow, easy punches. "Just like Flash, ha?"

"If you say so," says Emil, seeing no resemblance whatsoever between his father and the world-champ Filipino southpaw.

Francisco throws a few more combos. "I know I haven't been around much these last few years. I'm sorry for that. A boy needs his father."

Emil listens but doesn't say anything. How many times has he heard this apology only for Francisco follow it up with a tally of Emil's character flaws that could have been fixed if only Francisco had been around to guide him properly?

Except that is not what happens this time. Instead Francisco says, "But I'm proud of the man you've become."

Emil blinks, thrown off. His father's voice even sounds genuine.

"What a brain you have in that head of yours," Francisco adds as he continues striking the bag.

"Thank you?" Emil says, unsure where this is coming from, where it's going. This is, after all, the man who lectured him for wanting to take that advanced math class in junior high, for assuming Emil believes he's better than everyone else simply because he cares about his studies.

"Me and your mother and your auntie Carmen were talking last night. About your plans after you graduate high school."

Ah, here it comes, the part where his father tells him more education is a waste of time.

"And," Francisco continues, "we were wondering where you had your heart set on for college." Francisco throws a flurry of punches that jolts Emil's body through the bag.

Emil steps back and stands up straight. "*You* actually want me to go to college?"

"Sure. You'd be the first in our family—on either side."

Emil blinks.

Francisco throws a lazy left hook. "You seem surprised."

"The way you've always talked about educated Filipinos, I always thought . . ."

"What?"

Emil hesitates.

"Go on," Francisco encourages.

Emil rubs the back of his neck and looks down. "That you hated them. That you think they're traitors."

"No, no, no, no. I mean, kind of. But no, of course not."

"Really?" asks Emil, remembering all the times his father has referred to college-educated Filipinos as *capitalist lapdogs*.

"I don't hate any man for his education, Emilio. But I do hate what most seem to do with that education." Francisco puts his gloves back up, and Emil leans into the bag again.

"What do you mean?"

"I hate those who believe it makes them superior to people who've never had the same opportunities," Francisco says, throwing a jab with his left, followed by a right cross. "Those who feel ashamed of their ancestors who paved the way." Cross, left hook, cross. "Those who believe a man's worth is determined by the size of his bank account or the title in front of his name." Jab, cross, hook. "Those who ignore the suffering of their brothers." Jab, cross, left uppercut, cross. "Those who would rather become the oppressor than fight the oppression." Jab, jab, jab. "Those like your auntie." He grins behind his gloves. "Joke lang."

This is a distinction Emil has never heard his father make explicit before, one that shifts and softens his attitude. "I don't know where I want to go to college yet," he says, stepping back from the bag once more.

Francisco lowers his fists, breathing hard now. He grabs a towel, wipes the sweat off his forehead, and tosses it aside. "Just make sure you use what you learn for the people, Emilio. For the movement. Imagine all the good you could do. Be Prometheus."

"Huh?"

"Steal fire." Francisco winks. "See, your old man knows a few things even if he didn't go to college."

"Then my old man must also know the gods doomed Prometheus to an eternity of an eagle devouring his liver as punishment."

"That's beside the point."

"Is it, though?"

"The movement needs everyone," Francisco says, undeterred but slipping into his activist voice. "The striking workers, of course. But also writers, artists, musicians, accountants, cooks, teachers, engineers, janitors, journalists, lawyers, city planners, doctors, taxi drivers, real estate agents, housewives, and everyone else. It takes more to change the world than signs and speeches." Francisco closes the space between them and rests a gloved fist on his son's shoulder. "You haven't been to a strike since you were a little boy. You're a man now. Come with me when I return to Delano this time. See it up close for yourself. See where you fit in, what you might do."

"I don't know," Emil says, because he can't help but think of all the things that never seem to cross Francisco's mind. With both him and his father gone, how will his mother pay the family's bills on her wages alone? Will Auntie Carmen hold his job at the café? If not, who else will hire him, and how will he save enough for tuition? And what about school, which starts in a few weeks?

"This isn't going to be any old strike, Emilio. It's going to change things, change history. Forever. I want you to witness that. To be part of that."

"Won't the Mexicans cross the picket line as usual?" Emil asks, grasping for a logical reason to deny Francisco's request.

"Not this time." Francisco steps back, shakes out his arms. "Mang Larry has been talking to Chavez, Huerta, and their other leaders. He's confident he can convince them to join the strike—then we'll form a real agricultural workers union. One that can speak with a single voice, that will be so big, so powerful, that the growers will have no choice but to listen or let their harvests rot."

If this is true, that's huge. But Emil is well-versed in how his father tells people what they need to hear to change their minds.

"Their imperialism brought us to this country as a source of cheap labor, anak." Francisco goes on before Emil can answer, fists back up. "They never intended for us to stay. So we must fight for our place. Come, see how we fight. See what a revolution really takes."

TO LEAVE

Emil does not go with his father when he leaves a few days later—but neither does Emil refuse the money Francisco offers for a bus ticket should Emil change his mind.

"Do you think you'll go?" Emil's mother asks in the quiet of their kitchen after the door clicks closed behind Francisco. She's at the sink, smoking a cigarette and cleaning up after her husband before heading off to the hotel to clean up after less familiar strangers.

Emil is at the table finishing his tortang talong and pretending to read the latest issue of *Anak ng Bukid* that his father left on the table. He shrugs, then asks without looking up, "Do you think I should?"

"Do you want to?"

Emil shrugs again. His conversation with Francisco the other day in the gym didn't convert him to the cause, but it piqued his curiosity.

"Just remember," his mother says, "to leave is to leave something behind."

He understands that she does not only mean his job or his studies or their bills. She does not only mean his Sunday mornings on the banks of the San Joaquin.

No. She also means the fragmented lives. Lovers who will lay their heads down next to empty pillows. Children who will never comprehend how their father's departure could be anything other than an escape.

No matter the reason, no matter how practical or noble—Emil understands all the way down to his marrow what his mother means. Both have been among those things Francisco leaves each time he goes away to play hero to the people. It would be impossible for Emil to be away for any significant length of time himself without guilt gnawing at his heart.

However, maybe he doesn't need to *stay* in Delano for any significant length of time. He could ask Auntie Carmen for one of the slow days off, then go down in the morning, see what's what, and return on the midnight bus. Maybe his father is right and Emil would see things differently now that he is a man. Maybe not.

Emil finishes his breakfast, thanks his mother, kisses her goodbye.

❧

Several Filipinos catch Francisco's fire and head south to Delano in the following days. Not enough to cause any great shift in Little Manila or in the labor force it provides the area. But enough that it does not go unnoticed.

To some, it's simply one more seasonal move; to others, a chance to finally do something significant, to sow a seed not meant for white mouths.

Dark, Dark, Dark

Later that week, Emil is sitting on a milk crate in the alley behind the café, taking a break after the dinner rush. The stink of garbage that's absorbed the heat of the day radiates from the overflowing dumpster while the sky glows orange with the sunset. Up and down the street echo the conversations, laughter, and arguments of gamblers and pool players only just beginning their evenings.

Emil leans forward, elbows on knees. In one hand, a cigarette. In the other, the folded bills his father handed him for bus fare. Auntie Carmen had—reluctantly—agreed to let him have tomorrow off, so in the morning, he'll be on his way to Delano.

Even though he doesn't plan to be gone for long, he can't help but remember the exhausted, resigned expression on his mother's face when he told her. Their entire lives, Francisco's presence has been fleeting, like a firefly's glow erratically pulsing in the night. Now here. Now there. Now here again. Now there again. Now dark, dark, dark until you're sure it's gone for good.

And now here is her son, blinking out of existence. Temporarily, he assured her, but maybe his assurances sounded like an echo of his father's.

The building's back door pops open, startling Emil into dropping the money. He picks it up and pockets it as his cousin Leon, Auntie Carmen's oldest, steps outside. Leon leans back against the building next to

Emil and motions for a cigarette. Emil lights one and hands it over. Leon sticks it between his lips, crosses his thick arms over his broad chest, and starts talking as if continuing some conversation they'd been having from before.

Emil straightens his glasses and pretends to listen. It's either about cars or girls or basketball or drinking—all of which Leon seems to have infinite thoughts about; Emil, none.

The cousins have nothing in common beyond blood. Two years older than Emil, Leon would be a senior if he hadn't dropped out of high school when he was Emil's age to cook at the café full-time. Much to Auntie Carmen's dismay, his ambitions do not reach beyond the kitchen on the other side of the brick wall, beyond the Pinays in Little Manila and the south-side suburbs.

Leon wraps up his latest rant, then turns to Emil and says in English, "Heard you asked my mom for the day off tomorrow."

Emil puts out his cigarette and flicks it across the alley. Then he leans back against the brick wall. "Yeah."

"To go down to Delano."

It's not a question, so Emil doesn't bother responding. But he's not even sure how Leon knows that's his plan when he didn't share specifics with Auntie Carmen.

"Good," Leon says.

"Good?"

"You're planning to talk to your old man, right?"

"About what?"

Leon laughs. "About what? About how he's fucking things up for all of us."

"What's new?" Emil says with a shrug. It's not his job to rein his father in. And it's not like he even could if that was his goal instead of simply checking things out for the day.

"You notice how slow it was in there tonight?" Leon continues.

"Sure," Emil says, because although it wasn't dead, there aren't usually any open tables during the dinner rush like there were tonight.

"That's because of him."

"Not that many people followed him to Delano."

"Maybe not." Leon spits. "But people are taking their business down the block 'cause he's rocking the boat again. And since we're family, we're all about to fall out."

Emil doesn't say anything. The last of the sunlight dips below the horizon, and streetlights click on with their electric hums.

"Things have been pretty good for us, yeah?" Leon goes on. "Forget those old-timers still out in the fields. We've got some real roots now. My mom said there's even an immigration law about to go through, and we can start bringing more family over. And that law is also going to start letting in some more respectable Filipinos. Real professionals, you know? No more scraping the bottom of the barrel."

Emil had learned about this bill in school. His white history teacher had called it *the beginning of the end*. While Emil liked the man, the way he had glanced pointedly at Emil as he uttered those words made Emil shrink into himself, wishing he could disappear.

"Except," Leon says, "if people like your old man start up again with their strikes and whatnot, maybe those politicians will change their minds. Maybe they'll be afraid to let in any more of us."

"I don't think that's how it works."

"Hell, I didn't finish school and even I know that's exactly how it works, Emil. Thought you were supposed to be the smart one."

Emil clenches his jaw as he tilts his head back and stares at a cloud of insects hovering around a nearby light. "If it wasn't for my father, your family wouldn't even be here, Leon."

"Fuck that, little cousin. If it wasn't for mine, you and your mom would be sleeping in a closet in that rat-infested residential hotel where she scrubs shitters all day long." Leon takes one last drag, drops his cigarette onto the ground, and grinds it out with his heel. "Look. My point is this: Convince your old man to give up this nonsense when you see him tomorrow, or you can look for a new job when you step back off that bus."

Emil laughs, but Leon doesn't. He meets his cousin's gaze—and sees an actual threat. But is it his cousin's or his auntie's?

Either way, Emil burns at the betrayal. Except for work in the fields, jobs for a Filipino are hard to come by in this city. Isang bagsak, his ass. Family is only family until it affects the bottom line. Never mind how Francisco sent remittances to Auntie Carmen for years, paid for her to come to this country, gave her a place to sleep and food to eat, and found her a job and a husband. As soon as they bought a business and leased a building, Emil's family became little more than tenants to them.

Emil holds his cousin's gaze for a beat longer, then drops his eyes to the ground. "I'll see what I can do."

"Good boy." Leon pats Emil on the head as if he were a dog, then ducks back inside, letting the heavy door slam shut behind him.

Emil stands up, punches the wall, and kicks the milk crate, sending it clattering across the alleyway.

FRANCISCO

January 1930
Watsonville, CA

DRIFTWOOD

One of the manongs who had gone into the city brings Francisco his first letter from home. Having passed through many hands, it is faded and frayed. A minor miracle for proving he can still be found.

After dinner, he grabs a lantern and Lorenzo, who is one of the few men in the camp who can read and write. Francisco offers Lorenzo his usual fee, but his friend waves it away.

"Save it," Lorenzo says.

They find a quiet spot at the edge of a fallow field away from the low hum of the labor camp's evening conversation and card games. They sit down on a log in the oil lantern's orange glow. The evening's quickly cooled after winter's early sunset, and a misting drizzle hints at rain.

Lorenzo scans the letter, perhaps previewing the contents. As close as they are, Francisco bristles at the idea of someone else reading his family's words. But there's nothing to do but wait for his friend to translate the markings on the page and hope for accuracy, for good news.

"It's from your sister," Lorenzo says. "Dated April thirty."

Francisco nods, unsurprised. A year younger than him, Carmen is the only one in the family who can read and write, the only one still in school.

Lorenzo clears his throat and reads:

Dear Manong Isko,

I hope this letter finds you well. To be honest, Nanang's
upset that we've yet to receive any word from you . . . or any
money. But I tell her both are probably already on the way,
that it takes time to cross the world.

Since you left, Nanang's health has only gotten worse.
The coughing is very bad now, and she has become so weak
that she can no longer go into the city to sell her goods. She
spends most of the day lying down. The priest examined
her. His conclusion: Nanang has not properly atoned for
Tatang's adultery. His solution: a generous contribution to
the church. Of course!

Upon hearing this, Nanang threw a pot at the Spaniard
and said things that would not be proper for me to repeat
here.

Juan Luis and José help however they can, God bless
them, but they are still so young and able to do only so
much. Xavier continues to be Xavier. He has yet to accept his
responsibilities. Every day he seems to get into another fight,
and without you here, there's nobody he'll listen to. He asks
all the time when you'll return. I worry about what kind of
man he will become without one to teach him.

As for myself, I've had to stop attending school since
we could no longer afford it, so I spend most of my days
peddling in Nanang's place. The other day Sister Ana said

*I should be preparing to marry. I told her I was holding out
for one of your rich American friends!*

*In all seriousness, if I marry, who will hold our family
together? Sister Ana says it is by the grace of God that
we have enough to eat each day and that He will continue
to provide as He does for the birds. But when I point out
that it seems more to be the generosity of our neighbors,
who take turns bringing us a bit of food, she says it's the
same thing. Whether we're alive thanks to God or to our
neighbors, I don't think it will last much longer. Nobody
seems to have enough to spare these days.*

*To be honest, Manong, I really wish you would have
listened to Nanang and stayed. You abandoned us—
for what? You promised that you'll return—but when?*

*Perhaps you thought you could be one of the great
heroes out on an adventure to save the day. Perhaps
you were bored with our small barrio and wanted more.
Perhaps you were still angry at Tatang.*

*No matter the reason, I pray that you'll return.
Even if you become the richest man in America, will it
be worth it if we're not together, if we're not a family
anymore?*

*Maybe I'm being too harsh. If I'd been born a boy and
had any choice at all, I would have chosen to do the same,
especially after we lost the land, especially after everything
with Tatang.*

*Please take care of yourself, learn to write, then write us
as often as you can.*

*Though I know you do not like the church, remember
that God still loves you. I will pray for you every day.*

Dios ti agngina,
Carmen

After he finishes reading, Lorenzo is quiet. Many of the letters for the other men probably carried similar sentiments even if the details differed, so he knows to leave space for Francisco to feel these words that have arrived months after they were written, washing ashore like driftwood.

But when a long time passes and Francisco remains as still as stone, Lorenzo asks, "Would you like me to read it one more time, little brother?"

Francisco shakes his head.

"Would you like me to help you write a response?"

Francisco considers. The others often exaggerate and omit and out-right lie when writing home, sending photographs of themselves sharply dressed in borrowed clothes to bolster the deception about the success of their lives in America. Francisco doesn't want to lie, but neither can he bear the thought of sharing his humiliating reality, of admitting that after nearly one year, he has failed to save enough money to send home and that he's not sure how many more years it will take before he does have enough.

"Not yet," he says.

Lorenzo returns the letter.

Francisco breathes it in. Despite all the hands it passed through, the indescribable, sacred scent of home survived and, with it, all his sadness and love and anger and determination and regret.

He should never have left. He thought he was doing what was right, but maybe one of the reasons Carmen listed was the real reason. Maybe the decision was selfish, and now here he is stranded seven thousand miles from home.

Carmen wrote these words so many months ago—who knows what's happened since then? Who knows what will happen by the time he is finally able to return? Will Nanang still be alive? If not, will God forgive him?

You abandoned us—for what?

Head bowed as if in prayer, he listens to the sounds of the evening. The men rinsing their dishes, sweeping the dirt floors, straightening their things. A coughing fit. A burst of laughter. Someone strumming a guitar.

Francisco's heart wants to cry, but he refuses to let it. He must be strong.

After a while he clears his throat, refolds the letter, and stuffs it in his pocket. As if putting it away will stop his sister's words from replaying in his mind, will keep away the storm that's receded but not yet passed.

"Can I ask you something?" Francisco says.

Lorenzo nods.

"Do you ever wish you would have stayed home?"

Lorenzo considers the question. "I know you aren't going to stay, Isko, but I am. This is it for me."

"But is there any part of you that regrets coming?"

"My lolo often spoke about regret," he says. Lorenzo idolized his lolo, the man who'd raised him. A poet who'd survived the war with Spain only to be captured and tortured by the Americans a year later.

"And what did he say about it?" Francisco asks, as curious about the answer as much as what it must have been like to have a man in his life who spoke of and fought for things that mattered.

"That it's a useless word, Isko. That there's no going back, no changing what's in the past. Therefore, there's no use in spending too much time thinking about the past, in wishing you might have done something differently. A man should make his decisions and stand by those decisions, whatever the outcome. I decided America will be my new home, so America is my new home."

Francisco shifts. Moves the lantern over for no reason other than it's something to do with his hands. "I see."

"You don't sound convinced."

"It makes sense, Manong," Francisco says, the darkness outside the lamp's glow growing deeper. "But . . . I don't know."

"You feel regret?"

Francisco considers denying it, playing his question off as one of idle curiosity. Lorenzo just spoke about how men should never doubt themselves, so why lay his shame bare? But Francisco feels the need for honesty and trusts Lorenzo will not condemn him for it. So he nods.

Lorenzo sighs. "You thinking of going back soon, little brother?"

Francisco is quiet for a long time. "Maybe."

"Before the planting season?"

Francisco shrugs.

"Hmm." Lorenzo shifts but doesn't say anything else.

Francisco wants to ask if returning home with nothing would make him a failure of a man, but he doesn't want to force his friend to lie.

TRANSFORMATION

On Saturday night the transformation begins. The workers take turns bathing in the same water reheated over and over again by fire. They shave, polish shoes, slip on crisp McIntosh suits with padded shoulders and wide lapels. They smooth eyebrows, slick back straight black hair, straighten silk ties, and crown themselves with fedoras. Finally they fill their pockets with as much cash as they can afford to not send home. Okay, maybe just a bit more than that because it's a dime a dance, and there are tips and drinks, and they're not stingy.

Nearly all the single men—and a few of the married ones—join the ritual even if they don't like dancing, but who doesn't like dancing? The first ones ready—usually the Visayans—cram into the jalopies and ride over, leaving the rest to walk. But there's safety in numbers, so nobody walks alone. They are loud and incandescent as they tread west, the foothills behind them, until they reach the trolley line. They follow the tracks as they cut across the flat, manure-scented fields and into town. Every now and then a car clangs past, and the men fall quiet until it's gone, each one pretending that it doesn't bother them that they're not allowed to ride in it, pretending not to notice the POSITIVELY NO FILIPINOS ALLOWED placards hanging in the windows of storefronts and hotels, which even those who can't read have learned to recognize.

Francisco and Lorenzo linger in the back of a quieter group of

Ilokanos. Francisco rolls up the sleeves of the oversized suit he pulled from the shared closet. The evening's a ripe fruit ready to be plucked and eaten right off the branch, because tonight's particularly special: a pair of Ilokanos has leased the new dance hall, so the money they spend will be going to their own for once.

"You going to mix it up this time?" Lorenzo asks in English so they can practice the clunky language. "Or you still sticking with that blond all night—what's her name? Mary or something? The one you always manage to find no matter the hall?"

"Milly." Francisco laughs. "But it's not like that, Manong."

"Oh, then what's it like, little brother?" Lorenzo reaches over and tucks in the back of Francisco's shirt collar.

Francisco shrugs. "She's a good dancer. We have fun."

"Right. *Fun.*"

"Don't say it like that."

"Like what?"

"You know. Like you don't believe me."

"Well, little brother, whatever you and Mary are doing, I definitely believe you're having fun!" Lorenzo moves to ruffle Francisco's hair, but he shoves Lorenzo away, laughing.

"Milly, not Mary."

"Just be careful, Isko," Lorenzo says, tone shifting. "Remember Perfecto."

As if any of them could forget. Despite the law, Perfecto and his girl, Esther, had fallen in love and gotten engaged. But the good white people of Watsonville could not abide one of their daughters being seduced by a brown-skinned field laborer. Just over a month ago, the police raided his boardinghouse and found the two of them together, along with Esther's younger sister, then made Perfecto out to be some pervert preying on the girls. They claimed he was older than he was and skipped over the fact that Perfecto had simply agreed to help Esther care for her younger sister like their mother had wanted.

Now the girls had been returned to parents who didn't want them, Perfecto sat in prison awaiting trial, more NO FILIPINOS AND NO DOGS signs had gone up around town, and more white men were attacking Filipinos if they caught them alone.

"We're just dancing, is all," Francisco says.

"Sure, sure. Just remember that you're only sixteen. Dance all you can with as many girls as you can. Dance all night."

That had been Francisco's tatang's approach. It would not be his.

They soon reach the end of the trolley tracks, where the new dance hall sits perched on low bluffs among clumps of golden seagrass that rustle in the evening's salty breeze. Light and music spill from the windows. The ocean churns, unseen, in the darkness below.

As the men approach the entrance, smiles widen and eyes brighten. They remove hats, check hair, and jostle through the door, hoping their knives or balisongs are hidden well enough so as not to be confiscated.

"Ladies, ladies, ladies," one of the men calls from ahead in English as they step into the noise and light and smoke. "I have arrived, so the party may begin! Who would like to be blessed with my first dance?"

Francisco and Lorenzo enter last. They check their jackets and follow the others upstairs to where the band is playing "Ain't Misbehavin'" while couples dance on the freshly waxed floor. Greetings and laughter and professions of love fight for airspace over the music. A few of the men head straight for the bar at the back, but Francisco and Lorenzo join the rest in the ticket seller's line. The men bob to the beat as they wait, scanning the spinning skirts and arguing over who will get to dance with which girl next. Most of the girls are young—Okies or Europeans—but there are a handful of Mexican girls and even Mang Carlos's two mestiza daughters, despite the community's judgment.

Lorenzo drifts away as Francisco searches for Milly's long blond hair and tries to suppress thoughts of taking her away to somewhere like New Mexico, where it's legal for them to marry. He reminds himself that this is temporary. It's a job for her. The men give their bodies to the fields while the women give theirs to the men.

Francisco buys his tickets as the song ends and the whistle blows, indicating it's time for new partners. Yet Francisco still can't find Milly by the time the opening notes of "Am I Blue?" reach into the air.

A white girl with brown hair and freckles in a long green skirt sashays up to him. "You're looking for Milly, right?" she asks with a Southern accent.

He doesn't recognize this girl—how does she know?

Reading his surprise, she explains, "You're always looking for Milly."

"I guess I am," Francisco says in English. He turns his attention back to the crowd. "But I don't see her. Will she come later?"

The girl shakes her head. Smiles. "Forget about her. I've always thought you were real cute for a brown fella, so how about you spend some of those tickets on me? Spend enough and maybe—"

Francisco's face falls. "Why isn't she coming?"

"She's done, darling."

"Done?"

"Yup."

Francisco's heart sinks. "Why?"

"Her daddy said no more."

"She's never coming back?" Francisco asks.

The brown-haired girl shakes her head, then shifts her attention to another man, concluding accurately that Francisco's a lost cause. Sure enough, Francisco heads over to the bar, orders a drink, and takes it outside onto the deck that overlooks the beach.

It's still early enough in the evening that he has the deck to himself. He sets his beer on the railing and lights a cigarette. As he takes the first drag, he leans over the railing and watches the whitecaps roll through the darkness while the music pulses behind him. Overhead, the stars shine bright through the crisp winter air.

In between drags, he takes a drink and enjoys the way the alcohol warms his stomach.

Okay. Maybe he lied to Lorenzo. Maybe he hadn't simply been dancing with Milly all these nights. Maybe he had been starting to imagine a new shape to things when he began to realize it was going to take much longer than he thought to make the kind of money he needs to take care of his family. Maybe he'd started to believe he and Milly could have some kind of future together. Despite California law. Despite the town. Despite the fact he hadn't even known where she lived or if Milly was even her real name, since it isn't unheard of for the girls to invent new selves here.

It was real, wasn't it, the way she always sought him out as soon as he arrived? The way she never stopped smiling at him? The way she placed her hand on his chest when she laughed at his jokes or the way he pronounced certain English words?

It doesn't matter now. She's gone. One less reason to linger.

From within the dance hall, a song ends, the whistle blows, and there's the scramble to find new partners. As the band starts playing again, the back doors open. Light, sound, and smoke spill into the night, then recede. Footsteps approach, and a girl appears at his side.

"You mind?" she asks in Ilokano.

Before Francisco can answer, the girl uses his shoulder to hoist herself onto the railing. She swings around so she's sitting next to him and facing the sea, crosses her legs, and straightens her long dark blue skirt.

"Can I get one of those?" she asks, holding out her hand.

It's Mang Carlos's older daughter, the one who helps her mother cook at the labor camp. Stray strands of her long black hair have escaped from her bun. Sweat trickles down the side of her brown face, which is a blend of her mother's Mexican features and her father's Filipino ones. Her dark eyes bore into him, bright and curious.

He passes her a cigarette. She places it in her mouth and leans over so he can light it. He strikes a match, cupping his hand to protect the small flame from the wind, then lights the cigarette. The orange tip brightens with her first inhale.

"You're Beatriz Roxas, right?" he asks.

"Call me Bea." She helps herself to his drink. "And you're Isko Maghabol."

He nods, surprised. There are so few women in the camp that everyone knows them, but there were so many men, he assumed that to her, he was one more face in a constantly shifting crowd.

"My tatang loves you," she explains.

"He does?" Francisco drops his gaze, embarrassed for some reason.

"Sure. Says there's something in you. A fire."

"What does that mean?"

She shrugs.

"Shouldn't you be in there dancing, Bea?" Francisco says so they'll stop talking about him.

"Shouldn't you, Isko?"

"It costs me money."

"And who's to say it doesn't cost me something too?"

"Fair enough."

He snatches his drink back. She takes a drag.

"We've never danced together, Isko."

"True."

"Want to know why I think that is?" She goes on without waiting for his answer. "I think you're one of these fools driven crazy by the sight of pale skin and yellow hair."

He shakes his head as he takes a drink.

She laughs. "Oh, so you're denying it? I've seen you around these dances and noticed you only go with that one blond girl with the annoying laugh."

"Her laugh's not annoying."

Beatriz raises her eyebrow but says nothing. Francisco almost smiles.

"Tell me, what is it about them? My sister thinks it's because you boys believe they're all rich. But you'll tell me the truth, Isko, won't you?" She holds out her cigarette.

He takes a drag. She takes a swig. Then they trade back, smoke hanging in the cold air between them.

"I don't know, Bea," he says, telling the truth this time.

"Well, thanks for nothing." Beatriz laughs.

Francisco cracks a smile.

"Ah, there it is!" She pokes his cheek with the pinky of the hand holding the cigarette. "I knew I could get one out of you."

They stay that way for a while, her sitting on the railing and him leaning next to her. Her smoking, him drinking, occasionally swapping vices. Another song ends and the whistle trills.

"That's my cue." Beatriz swings back around and hops off the railing. She helps herself to the rest of his beer, then takes one final drag and passes the cigarette to Francisco to finish. "When you come back in, let's have a dance."

"Maybe," he says. "If I go back in."

"But it won't be free," she says over her shoulder, and leaves him smiling a second time.

He lifts the beer to his lips, enjoying the suds sliding onto his tongue and the stars and the waves and the music swimming in his ears. He's forgotten every single word of the kundiman he'd started to compose in his head just a few minutes ago. Milly's already beginning to dissolve like a dream upon waking.

On the road in the distance, headlights approach, interrupting his peace. Curious to see who might be arriving this late, Francisco wanders over to the edge of the deck. The vehicle slows as it nears, and when it pulls up under the streetlamps, he tenses.

It's a faded blue pickup truck filled with white men. Two older ones up front in the cab, four older boys riding in the bed. They peer with disgust at the dance hall, bodies poised as if to hop out. Two in the back hold blackjacks and one a shotgun—which he suddenly aims at Francisco.

Francisco's breath hitches, and his stomach drops.

"Bang!" the boy shouts, then lowers the barrel to reveal a shit-eating grin.

One of them hurls something at Francisco. He ducks and covers his head as a glass bottle shatters against the side of the building.

The men laugh and howl like monkeys as the truck's engine roars to life, slipping back into the dark like an alligator sliding into the water.

Francisco's fear melts; then anger ignites. He spits in their direction, curses in Ilokano, and heads inside to find Beatriz for that dance.

THREE TYPES

"There are three types of Filipino men in America," Beatriz tells Francisco one night when they are walking together through an empty field. A crescent moon glows behind a thin haze of clouds. It's colder than usual, but neither notice.

"Kusto?" Francisco says, skeptical.

"I'm serious." She slaps his shoulder playfully. "I was born in a work camp and have lived my seventeen years surrounded by all of you, so I'm basically a researcher. No matter where I've been—whether it's the Yakima or Wenatchee or Central or Imperial Valleys—there are always three types of you."

"Ilokanos, Visayans, and Tagalogs?"

Beatriz rolls her eyes. "No, you fool. Doesn't matter where you're from."

"Don't keep me waiting."

"Okay, first, there are those rooted in the past. The serious ones who work and save, work and save. They speak only in their dialects and only with those from the same province, exchanging memories and news and chismis. They stay behind when the others go to the dance hall. They stay behind when the rest of you go to town or mass or the beach or the picnics or the cockfights."

"True enough." Francisco can easily name the men who fit such a description.

Beatriz goes on. "They've accepted that their lives are a sacrifice for their families back home, to whom they send nearly all their earnings. They speak as if they will one day follow their money across the sea, even though they know they won't."

"That's one type," Francisco says as they pass two men practicing eskrima, their bamboo sticks clacking rhythmically under the moonlight. "How about the other two?"

"The second are those who stake their claim in the present. They spend, spend, spend, and speak, speak, speak. They speak of the brown girls they left waiting and the white girls they'll dance with this Saturday night. Of the trim and cut of their suits. Of the cars they share and the one they'll buy if they send a bit less home this month and the next and probably the next year or two, to be honest. Of how much they can drink. Of the card games and cockfights they won—but not of those they lost. Of the men they'll supposedly kill."

Francisco nods, loving the way her mind weaves words from thoughts. "I know many men like this. Afraid of stillness. Afraid that to stop would mean to stop being."

"Finally," Beatriz continues, needing no reassurance that she's right, "there are those who tether themselves to the future. They work and dance and pray and fish and fight just enough to survive. But mostly they save and save and save. They also search for wives, not caring about the color of their skin or where they're from or if they even speak the same language. They place their faith in our wombs, praying for children who might one day make something of themselves, for themselves, in this country, broken and imperfect as it is. Something with teeth so this self-imposed exile will have been worth it."

"Your tatang?" Francisco says, picking up a rock and then tossing it into the darkness of the field.

She nods.

"And what about the men who go back home?" he asks.

She laughs. "None of you go back home."

Francisco puts his hands in his pockets. It is certainly starting to seem that way. "Which type of man do you think I am?"

"None of them," Beatriz says, smirking. "You're still a boy, Isko."

"You're very funny, Bea. You know that?"

"And intelligent. And beautiful. The combination's a burden, really."

"Anyway, if you won't tell me which type I am, at least tell me which you think is best. Which type will you marry?"

Beatriz gives Francisco a playful elbow to the ribs. "Who says I want to marry?"

"You don't?"

"Maybe. Maybe not."

"What else would you do?"

"A woman can be more than someone's wife, you know."

"Sure, she can be someone's mother," he jokes.

The joke does not land. Instead Beatriz dims, grows quiet.

As they continue walking, Francisco wishes he could turn back time and keep his mouth shut. "Sorry," he says eventually.

She looks up, gazes into the distance, shrugs.

"I think you're onto something with your theory," Francisco says, trying to steer the conversation back to safe ground. "But I think you need to continue your study. I believe there might be many more types of men yet to be discovered."

They keep walking. Beatriz still doesn't say anything.

"And what about the women?" Francisco tries.

She turns to him, skeptical. "What about them?"

"What are the different types of Filipinas here in America?"

"Ha. You'll have to figure that out for yourself." Beatriz lets a small smile escape. "That is, if you can peel your eyes away from blond girls long enough to notice any of us."

They laugh again, then lapse back into silence, but this time a comfortable one. The clouds shift. Rain begins to mist, enough that Francisco drapes his jacket over Beatriz's head but not enough that they stop walking. Her hair tickles his nose, smelling of campfire smoke and soap.

He wonders what type of man he wants to be. What type he will be.

SOUTHBOUND

A few days later, Francisco returns from another failed job search to find Beatriz's family's cabin empty. After asking the men who live next door, he learns that Mang Carlos feared trouble was brewing—too many Communists had been coming around the farms, too many white women had been coming around the dance halls, and too many Filipinos had been coming to this country. So after news spread of the latest Filipino found beaten bloody, the old man made his family pack what they could carry and shepherded them onto a southbound freight train.

Francisco returns to the small cabin to search for something that looks like a goodbye note from Beatriz. There's nothing, of course. He sits down on the worn wooden frame of the open doorway and leans forward, elbows resting on his knees. One by one, he cracks his knuckles.

He should already be used to this by now. None of them stayed anywhere for long in this country. In only a year, how many different places had he himself slept in? How many different jobs had he worked? How many people had he met, then lost?

Some he'll see again, but others disappear without a goodbye. It's impossible to know which will be which. Everything is seasonal.

"Excuse me, young man," someone says in Ilokano, interrupting Francisco's thoughts. It's an old-timer with a sun-faded face, carrying a duffel bag and a black rooster. "I was told this cabin is available, ha?"

"Sorry," Francisco says. "It is." He stands up and moves out of the way. The man nods, steps inside, and shuts the door.

Francisco takes one last look at Beatriz's former cabin, then wanders off in a random direction. Maybe it is time to return home. He loses a piece of himself each time he leaves or each time someone he loves leaves him. If he stays for even just a few more years and continues to live this life of constant reset, what will eventually remain?

ENZO

March–April 2020
Philadelphia, PA

THOR AND HIS INFINITE BLADDER

As spring arrives in fits and starts despite the way time seems to have stopped, Enzo continues to ask Lolo Emil if he wants company on his evening walks, even though Lolo Emil continues to say no.

"It's okay to give up," Chris quietly tells Enzo one night as they set the table together while a handmade bulgogi pizza bakes in the oven. Julia's grading in her office. Lolo Emil is in the living room watching a reality show about couples who get engaged before ever seeing each other and wondering aloud why Chris can't make a "normal" pizza. It's Enzo's spring break, but it doesn't feel any different with nobody going anywhere, the entire world in a holding pattern.

"I know," Enzo says.

"But you're going to keep asking, aren't you?"

"Probably."

"Why?" Chris glances toward the living room and shakes his head. "He's a lost cause."

Enzo shrugs as he pours the waters. It's a good question, one he asks himself each time Lolo Emil pushes back from the table, steps into his shoes, and clips on Thor's leash. One Enzo still doesn't know the answer to.

At first he thought Lolo Emil was simply the type of person who needed to be asked more than once. After a week of the old man saying no, Enzo's brain told him to stop asking. But another part of Enzo compelled him to continue. Whether it was for Lolo Emil's sake or his own, he couldn't say.

So tonight, after they finish dinner, Enzo asks again.

Lolo Emil doesn't respond as he steps into his shoes and slips on his jacket. Thor climbs down from the living room couch, stretches, and shakes himself out. But instead of going to the door like usual, the dog trots over to Enzo and nuzzles against his legs.

Lolo Emil calls for Thor, but he stays with Enzo, blissing out as Enzo scratches him behind the ears. The old man sighs. "Fine. Come."

"Really?" Enzo asks, exchanging surprised glances with his parents.

Lolo Emil zips up his jacket. "Just for tonight. Then you stop pestering me about it."

"Can you wait for me to wash the dishes?"

Instead of answering, Lolo Emil walks over, clips on Thor's leash, and leads him away.

Enzo looks to his parents. Julia gestures for him to go. "Your dad will take care of them."

Chris raises his eyebrow. "I will?"

"You will," Julia confirms.

"Fine." He turns to Enzo. "But you owe me."

"Deal." Enzo hops out of his chair, puts on a surgical mask, and rushes out the front door.

It's a warm, clear evening. Still light out. The street's lined with parked cars that haven't moved in who knows how long, petals from the flowering cherry blossom and almond trees carpeting their windshields. The scent of a neighbor cooking some spiced meat hangs in the air.

Lolo Emil and Thor haven't made it very far, so Enzo easily catches up with them. Thor is sniffing one of the young maple trees planted in a small square patch of dirt cut into the sidewalk two houses down. Neither the old man nor the dog acknowledges Enzo's presence, so Enzo walks up without saying anything.

Thor lifts a leg, pees against the tree, then continues, Lolo Emil and Enzo trailing behind his gently wagging tail. But it's not long before the old black dog stops to sniff the next tree and relieve himself again.

"Is the entire walk going to be like this?" Enzo asks.

"He's a dog," Lolo Emil says. "It's the sniffing that stimulates his brain, not the walking."

"Oh." Enzo slips his hands into his hoodie pocket.

They walk. Thor sniffs the next tree. Pees. Trots ahead.

"How is there any urine left in his bladder?" Enzo asks.

"Eric," Lolo Emil says, "you don't need to fill the air with words all the time."

"Yeah. Sure. My bad, Lolo."

They continue in this stuttering manner, following Thor and his infinite bladder from tree to tree. The sun sinks slowly behind the row houses. The wind rustles the leaves. A delivery truck rumbles past. Neighbors nod or wave from stoops, already familiar with the sunset sight of the old brown man and his old black dog.

Enzo does indeed feel the need to fill the air with words. This is supposed to be his opportunity to finally speak with his grandfather like his dad wanted. There's also something about being under a cloudless sky that always makes Enzo want to open up. Maybe it's that there's space to breathe, to stretch, to be. The sense that whatever is said or shared won't linger, won't suffocate, but instead will burn off into the atmosphere and drift away.

Yet the sky must not have the same effect on Lolo Emil. Block after block, he doesn't utter a single word. He watches Thor, nods to the neighbors, periodically checks the sky. When Thor poops on the curb, he wordlessly hands Enzo a small green plastic bag. Enzo tries to hand it back, but Lolo Emil just points to the poop until Enzo picks it up.

"This is messed up," Enzo mumbles, then holds his breath as he ties off the bag and tosses it in the nearest garbage bin. "You're welcome," he tells the dog.

The dog says nothing.

"Why did you decide to let me walk with you if you don't even want to talk?" Enzo asks after a few more blocks.

"Isn't it obvious?"

"No."

"So I don't have to pick up shit anymore."

◗

The next day after dinner, Lolo Emil surprises everyone by telling Enzo from the doorway, "I don't have all night, Eric—get your shoes on."

So Enzo joins him and Thor again.

"Can I hold his leash?" Enzo asks once they're outside.

"No," Lolo Emil says. "But here are the poop bags."

They're quiet the rest of the way.

◗

Enzo walks with Lolo Emil and Thor again the following night. The conversation embargo still in place, Enzo checks his phone after a few blocks. Not a single notification or text. Not even from Kyle.

Lolo Emil grunts with disapproval. "Put that thing away."

"Sorry," Enzo says. "It's just that it's been a couple days since I've heard from my best friend. He has a lot of friends, so sometimes I feel like he forgets about me."

"'Best friend'? Are you a girl now?"

Enzo half laughs, unsure if the old man's being serious. "What, guys can't have close friends?"

Lolo Emil says nothing. Thor stops to sniff a flamingo garden decoration. A helicopter passes overhead. Enzo notices a flowering cherry blossom tree at the corner and walks ahead to snap a picture.

"Your generation and your phones," Lolo Emil complains as he and Thor catch up to Enzo, who's staring at the screen, testing different filters on the photo. "For crying out loud, put it away. You're not going to die if you don't look at it for thirty minutes."

"I know," Enzo says without looking up. "It would probably take at least an hour."

Lolo Emil shakes his head, almost smiling.

❧

The next walk, Enzo leaves his phone at home to test Lolo Emil's theory.

"See," Lolo Emil says when they return, "you're still here."

Enzo presses two fingers to his wrist to check his own pulse. "Just barely."

Lolo Emil laughs. Briefly.

❧

Spring break ends. Enzo continues to leave his phone at home when they walk each night. Not because his lolo told him to. Not to test a theory. But because he comes to appreciate the way he notices more without it. He notices the shifting scents in the air, the subdued sounds of a city in quarantine, the changing phases of the moon. He notices the neighbors that sit out on their stoop each night, the blossoming trees and the trees with budded branches ready to blossom, the house on the corner where there's always a black cat in the window, the house two blocks over where someone's always listening to the Roots.

And he notices that Lolo Emil has learned the neighbors' names, that he picks up the litter he comes across, that he kisses Thor's nose at the start and end of each walk.

The maddening buzz of Enzo's mental murder hornets begins to quiet. Not completely, and not all the time. But for the length of the walk and a bit afterward. Enough to relax, enough to focus, enough to be more than a hive of anxiety worrying about a world on fire.

❧

"How was the walk?" Chris asks one night. He's sitting on the living room couch with a documentary in Tagalog on the TV.

"Good," Enzo says, wandering over as Lolo stomps up the stairs to his room.

When Lolo Emil's footsteps fade and his door shuts, Chris says, "You know you don't have to keep going with him if you don't want to."

"Yeah, I know." Enzo watches a few seconds of the documentary, enough to figure out it's about the Philippine drug war. His anxiety begins to spike at the thought of all the dead, so he turns away. "I actually like it."

"You do?"

"Yeah."

Chris lowers his voice. "I can't even imagine spending that much time with that man voluntarily. What do you guys even talk about?"

"Nothing."

"That doesn't surprise me. But are *you* okay with that?"

"Sure."

Chris raises an eyebrow. "Really?"

"I guess."

Chris turns his attention back to the screen. "If you say so."

*

The next night, when a light rain is falling and the sun is still glowing low on the horizon behind thin clouds, Enzo asks Lolo Emil, "What was your relationship like with your grandparents?"

Lolo Emil coughs and coughs, then hocks up a wad of phlegm. As clear as his throat may now be, no words pass through it.

Enzo wonders if he's ruined this fragile thing they've formed. After a few more silent blocks, he's sure that he has, that tomorrow Lolo Emil will want to go back to walking alone. Why couldn't he be content with simply walking? Why did he let his dad's question get to him?

But then the old man speaks, voice quieter than usual. "Normal, I suppose. At least with my mother's parents. We got along all right. Saw one another at the holidays."

"Her mom was Mexican, right?"

He nods. "And her father was Filipino. Making her what they call Mexi-pina now."

"¿Ella hablaba español?" Enzo asks.

"Of course," Lolo Emil says.

"Did she teach you to speak it?"

"What would have been the point?"

"Right. And what about your dad's parents?" Enzo asks. "What was your relationship like with them?"

Lolo Emil shrugs. "They lived in the Philippines, so I never knew them. Besides, my grandfather left my father's family when he was just a boy. Then he came to this country when he was fifteen and never looked back."

"You never met them?" Enzo asks.

Lolo Emil clears his throat and spits again. "Don't even know their names or where exactly they were from."

Enzo already knows as much. Chris has spent hours on Facebook trying in vain to find living relatives on his dad's side, hoping to visit them in real life someday, but it's impossible to confirm if those who share their surname are actual relatives without those crucial facts.

They're quiet for a while. Then Enzo decides to push his luck. "And what about your dad—did you guys get along?"

Chris—being a history teacher—always made sure Enzo knew the man was a hero in the farm labor movement on the West Coast. When he would come across a well-researched article or book that actually addressed the contributions made by those beyond the Mexican American organizers, Chris would read it aloud to Enzo. Sure enough, his great-grandfather's name—Francisco Maghabol—would appear alongside the other important manongs of the movement: Larry Itliong, Benjamin Gines, Pete Velasco, and Philip Vera Cruz. But Chris never had much personal knowledge to pass on.

Lolo Emil scoffs. "He was barely a father."

"What do you mean?"

The rain picks up. Lolo Emil opens his umbrella. "The man struggled to hold a steady job, so our family was dirt-poor. If it wasn't for my mother and me working all the time and my auntie's help, who knows if we would have had anything to eat at all."

"Oh," Enzo says, surprised, opening his own umbrella now. His dad never told him about this.

"But he probably didn't know how to be a father because his own was such a deadbeat. For crying out loud, a man doesn't up and leave his wife and kids like that. No matter what. That's the whole point of being a man."

Enzo waits for Lolo Emil to say more, but he leaves it at that. There's a sad heaviness to the silence that indicates the old man's done talking, so Enzo decides not to push it any further. They walk on, listening to the falling rain.

Night by night and block by block, Enzo and Emil begin to talk.

Lolo Emil tells Enzo about growing up in Stockton, California. About attending the only integrated school in town, working at his aunt's restaurant, and studying whenever he could. About his father forever causing trouble, sharing a tiny apartment with a rotating string of random laborers, not having enough to eat.

He tells Enzo about falling in love with Enzo's grandma Linda on the first day of college—and about finding out she was pregnant a few months later. About her family's anger and its fierce blossoming the day they found out the baby's father was not white. About marrying at the courthouse the following week. About continuing with his studies and working multiple jobs to support their family while she dropped out to care for baby Christopher. About finally earning the lukewarm approval of Linda's family by finishing at the top of his class and landing an engineering position right after graduation that paid more in one year than his parents probably made in a decade, a job that he would keep until his retirement. About continuing to send his own mother money each month until the day she died.

He tells Enzo about loneliness and how it seems to multiply with each passing year. Losing his parents, his friends, Grandma Linda. Growing more and more distant from his children and grandchildren. Then finding Thor through a senior dog adoption organization that worked with his retirement home and feeling a bit less lonely.

And Enzo tells Lolo Emil about growing up in Philly. About how his earliest memories are of reading English and Tagalog and Spanish children's books with his parents. About his private Montessori elementary school and then the shock of public middle school. About how his family took turns choosing the music they listened to during dinner. About strict screen time policies, reading hour, Taco Tuesday, Friday-night pizza, and Saturday-morning housecleaning. About fall camping trips in the Adirondacks, weekend trains to New York to catch Broadway plays, Memorial Days at the edge of the Atlantic Ocean. About two weeks each summer spent with his dad's friends in the Philippines or with his mom's side of the family in Puerto Rico, depending on the year. About how he's always wanted a dog, but his parents won't let him get one.

He tells Lolo Emil about video games and TV shows and art and basketball. About his athletic, popular friend Kyle who's into healing crystals and yoga. About how he himself is not that athletic or popular and into neither healing crystals nor yoga but still likes Kyle because he's a good dude, even if he falls off the face of the Earth from time to time. About how his parents have always told him he could talk to either of them about anything but how he only completely feels like it's true about his mom. About his anxiety as murder hornets. About how he wants to make the world a better place but doesn't know how or if it's even possible. About the loneliness of being an only child—which Lolo Emil can relate to. About how he's always online thanks to his smartphone—which Lolo Emil suggests getting rid of.

Night by night, block by block, story by story, grandfather and grandson finally get to know each other in a way that's eluded so many of the men of their blood.

❧

"Do you really feel like you can't talk to your father?" Lolo Emil asks one night after Enzo admits as much. "You two seem to have a perfect relationship to me."

Thor's nails click along the cement. A clear orange sky hangs above dogwood trees heavy with blossoms. A young woman down the street is singing operatic scales in her living room.

"There's a lot we can talk about," Enzo says, holding Thor's leash. "School, my friends, TV, books, music, Filipino American history, current events. There are just some things . . . I don't know—I mean, I know he loves me. And I know he wants to be the kind of dad who can talk to his son about anything—he tells me that all the time. It's just that . . . I don't know. Never mind."

"Go on," Lolo Emil prompts.

Enzo hesitates. "You know how someone who's never done a certain thing can't really give you advice about that thing?"

"Like someone who's never fly-fished trying to teach you about fly-fishing?"

"I've never been fly-fishing before, but it's probably like that, I guess."

Lolo Emil stops suddenly, stricken. "Your dad's never taken you fly-fishing?"

"No."

"For crying out loud." Lolo Emil shakes his head. "I'll take you out someday, Enzo. Lots of good rivers over here."

"Cool," Enzo says.

They start walking again. "Anyway, you were saying?"

"Oh. Right. I was saying that Dad can talk to me about a lot, but he can't talk to me about anything too deep, too vulnerable. Like emotions. I guess because he's never learned to talk about his own."

"And you think that's important?"

"Of course it is. If you want to really get to know somebody, at least."

Lolo Emil scratches the side of his chin. He starts to say something, then pauses.

"What?" Enzo asks.

"Nothing."

"You wanted to keep talking, so now it's your turn."

"It's just . . ." The old man sighs. Stops to pet Thor. "That's probably my fault. In case you haven't noticed, he and I never really talked much. About anything, really. Not even surface things. And I don't think we were unique. That's how it was back then."

Enzo idly zips his jacket up and down as he keeps his eyes on the sidewalk, not knowing how to respond. It doesn't feel right to agree, even if he does.

"And it's not like I had someone to show me how either. The rare moments my father was home, he only spoke to me about his precious movement. Like I was his practice audience."

"Do you wish you would have been able to really talk to him?" Enzo asks. "To really have gotten to know him and have had him get to know you?"

"Sure. Some talks like this would have been nice. But I suppose nobody showed him how either." He chuckles. "We're like mirrors infinitely reflecting each other."

"Generational patterns," Enzo says. Dr. Mendoza talks about the concept all the time.

"That's a good term for it," says Lolo Emil.

"So why have we been able to talk so openly? What's different?"

Lolo Emil considers this. "Less history, maybe." He pauses a beat. "Fewer mistakes."

Then Enzo gets an idea. "What if we asked him to walk with us?"

"Your dad?"

"Yeah."

Shaking his head, Lolo Emil says, "I doubt he'd come."

"We can at least ask, right?"

"If you want," Lolo Emil says, then takes a deep breath like a diver preparing to plunge into ice-cold waters.

A MAN FOR ONCE

When Enzo asks if his dad wants to join their walk the next evening, surprise flashes across Chris's face. He glances at Lolo Emil, who looks away
without voicing an opinion on the matter. Then Chris turns back to Enzo.
"I'm not so sure this is a good idea, anak."

"Why not?" Enzo asks as Lolo Emil and Thor prepare to leave.

Chris starts to say something Enzo predicts will be an excuse but then
hesitates. He glances at Julia, who gives him a nearly imperceptible nod.
He sighs, grabs his jacket as if headed for the gallows.

The late-April sky is overcast. An unseasonably cold wind stirs the
leaves, blowing petals fluttering off their branches into the gutter and
sending litter skittering across the street. Enzo pulls on his stocking cap
and zips his jacket all the way up.

The sidewalk is too narrow for all three to walk side by side, so Enzo
and Lolo Emil walk next to each other as Chris trails behind. They pass the
first few blocks in awkward silence, buoyed by gusts of wind, Thor's sniffing, and their footfalls. Chris's presence changes the dynamic, and—as
Enzo worried might happen—the easy flow Enzo and Lolo Emil have
found these last few weeks falters.

"So," Enzo says, ready to break the ice, "I read this article the other day
about a new deep-sea fish oceanographers discovered."

They walk. Thor pees. Nobody asks any follow-up questions about the fish.

"I forget what it's called, but it's like . . ." He trails off.

They keep walking.

"Hey, Dad," Enzo tries, "how'd that Harlem Renaissance virtual museum project go with your classes?"

"What?" Chris asks. "I can't hear you from back here."

Enzo turns around and repeats his question while walking backward.

"Oh, it was fine. Some kids tried really hard and came up with some cool stuff. I can show you when we get home. Others . . . turned in absolutely nothing."

"That must make you feel really frustrated, right?"

Chris shrugs.

Enzo turns back around, disappointment on his face.

Lolo Emil notices. "Your son asked you a question, Christopher."

"And I answered it, Dad."

"No, you didn't."

"He knows what I meant. Right, Enzo?"

"Sure, Dad," Enzo says, pleading with his eyes for Lolo Emil to let it go. Thankfully he does. A fragile peace re-forms. They keep walking.

As they pass a vacant lot filled with broken bricks and blooming forsythia, Enzo decides to try again. "Lolo, how long were you and Grandma Linda married?"

"Forty-seven years," he answers without missing a beat.

"Wow," Enzo says. "What's the secret?"

"Patriarchy," Chris says dryly as he tucks a cigarette between his lips and lights it.

Lolo Emil sighs. Doesn't offer his own answer.

He's supposed to be Enzo's ally in this endeavor, though, so Enzo gives it another shot. "What was she like? I pretty much only knew her when she was sick."

A few moments pass, but Emil remains as talkative as a wall.

Chris exhales smoke, then smirks. "Your grandson asked you a question, Emilio."

Lolo Emil lets out another long-suffering sigh. "I don't feel like talking about her right now."

Enzo's shoulders sag. He slows down. "Maybe we should just go home?"

Lolo Emil gestures toward Thor. "He still needs to shit."

Silence returns. They keep walking.

When they reach the end of the next block, Lolo Emil, Thor, and Chris start to turn in the usual way. But Chris lingers at the corner.

Enzo notices after a few steps and stops. Lolo Emil and Thor do the same a moment later. They all turn to Chris.

"Everything okay, Dad?" Enzo asks.

Chris nods in the opposite direction. "We should go toward the park."

Lolo Emil scoffs. "At this hour?"

"It's well-lit."

"Do you want to get mugged?"

"Geez, Dad, it's not like that around here," Chris says, annoyed, sounding more like a teenager than Enzo.

"Let's let Thor decide," Enzo suggests.

All three watch the dog. He finishes urinating against the nearby tree and then lopes off in the usual direction he's been walking with Lolo Emil, away from the park.

Lolo Emil raises his eyebrow and follows Thor. Enzo waits for his dad.

"You know why he likes that dog so much better than he does the rest of us?" Chris says to Enzo but loud enough for Lolo Emil to hear. Enzo doesn't ask why, but that doesn't stop Chris from answering his own question. "Because he can train it to do whatever he wants." His tone suggests he's only half joking, real resentment simmering underneath the comment. "He only likes things he can control."

Lolo Emil stops suddenly, jerking Thor back. Once Thor sits obediently at his heels, he turns to Chris. "Is there a problem, Christopher? Is there something you'd like to say to me, or would you like to keep whispering behind my back like you're still some petulant child?"

"Forget it," Chris says, shaking his head and brushing past Enzo and Lolo Emil. "Let's just keep walking."

Enzo's not sure what to do, what to say. Maybe he should have prepped his dad before the walk. Or maybe he should let this play out. Maybe this is progress. Some things get worse before they get better, right? As uncomfortable as it is, his lolo and his dad are almost talking about something real for the first time in Enzo's life.

"Quit running away," says Lolo Emil, voice hardening. "Be a man for once."

Chris stops. Pauses. His anger emanates in waves as he keeps his back to them.

Enzo's chest tightens. Waits for his dad to quietly storm off.

But then, after a couple beats, Chris flicks his cigarette into the street, turns around, and strides back over, eyes narrowed, jaw set, fists clenched at his sides. The wind picks up, blowing his long hair all around his face.

"Want to know the problem?"

"Enlighten me."

"You—you're the problem and always have been. You're always trying to control everyone and everything around you. And so long as you can, you're happy. It's like when you made me quit football."

"Don't tell me you're still upset about that."

"I could give a thousand more examples."

"Please do."

"When I wanted to study history instead of engineering, when Amy and Jenny wanted to move to California, when Mom decided to stop chemo . . . You're always talking about how I run away, but don't you see that that's what you always do emotionally, mentally, when anyone makes a decision you can't control? What choice did any of us have but to leave when that's how you respond to us wanting to live our own lives?"

Enzo's heart is hammering, brain buzzing. It's hard to breathe. He starts to feel lightheaded, out-of-body. This is not at all how it was supposed to go.

Lolo Emil lets out an angry laugh. "'Emotionally'? Ah, here we go again—you always want to play victim. You need to invent some problem with me to justify your own discontent, your own failure. You ever think you wouldn't be so unhappy if you had chosen a career that actually paid enough so you could buy a real house in a decent neighborhood?"

Enzo's dad rubs his face hard, then shoves his fists into his pockets as if he might otherwise use them. "God, Dad, it always comes back to money with you! How can I get you to understand that that's not what everyone cares about? That's not what I care about! That's not what I want Enzo to care about!"

"Easy to say when you grew up with enough of it."

Tears well in Enzo's eyes. Thor's ears go back, and he starts to whimper as he edges closer to Enzo.

This is the exact opposite of progress, and Enzo doesn't know how to stop it from devolving even further. It's a battle he's watching from the rooftops.

"I can't talk to you!" Chris shouts.

"As if you ever tried," Emil says.

"I did!"

"When?"

"The day after Thanksgiving my sophomore year of high school," Chris fires back immediately, as if this bullet's been in the chamber for years.

"That's not what I remember about that day."

"No shit—you didn't listen. You never listen. Nobody can talk to you! You're so stuck in your own goddamn head that you can't see anything from anyone's perspective other than your own. But I guess you never could." Chris turns to Enzo as if remembering that he's there. "Sorry I ruined your walk," he says, voice softer, then heads back toward home.

Grandpa Emil tugs Thor's leash and strides away in their usual direction, as if nothing happened. Enzo is left alone on the street corner, surrounded by the rubble of a war that was waged long before he was born.

DOOMSCROLLING

Thor nudges Enzo's legs with his nose after dinner each night, but Enzo ignores the invitations. After that disastrous attempt to bring his dad along, he has given up on the walks. If nobody wants to speak to one another—to understand one another—then so be it. Instead he lies down on the couch with his noise-cancelling headphones and his phone and scrolls social media.

And as if to mirror his soul, the world worsens.

The United States seems on the verge of civil war over mask mandates and the closure of gyms. People hoard toilet paper. Businesses issue massive layoffs. Death rates climb. Each depressing news item nudges Enzo's soul closer to the abyss of complete cynicism.

The president continues calling the virus the "Chinese Virus," pronouncing the country's name in that odd way he does. And Enzo's social media feeds fill with stories and videos about people harassing or attacking random Asians and Asian Americans. Racist business owners saying racist shit, then denying entry or refusing service. Racist Lyft or Uber drivers refusing pickups. Racist coworkers moving their workstations. A pair of racist white teenage girls screaming, "Ewww!" and moving to the opposite end of a bus. Racist white people in passing cars throwing bottles. Random racists shouting things like "They should all be banned!" or "Go back to China!" or "You fucking immigrants!" Online racists filling social media with slurs. Racist attackers doing terrible things on videos Enzo can't bear to watch.

The victims are first-generation Americans and second and third and fourth. They are taking out their garbage, dining in a restaurant, buckling their baby's car seat, walking down the street, speaking their native language while on the phone, waiting for buses and trains. They are young, they are middle-aged, they are old. They are men and women and non-binary—but overwhelmingly they are women. They live in California and New York and nearly every state in between. They are Chinese and Korean and Vietnamese and Filipino and Japanese and Taiwanese and Hmong and nearly every other ethnicity under the "Asian" umbrella, because that is all it takes to be a target.

As if each viral story is not enough, Enzo's hope for humanity plummets even further as he reads the reports from Stop AAPI Hate tracking hate crimes against their community and learns they've been receiving nearly one hundred reports a day since their reporting center launched. One hundred. Each day. And what about the unreported, unrecorded?

Around the house, his mom tells the family about how the Puerto Rican economy is on the brink of collapse since it's still reeling from all the recent hurricanes and its complicated financial status as a commonwealth territory. His dad rants about the Philippine government's strict lockdown measures but lack of testing and support for those who can't go to work. He goes off on how when people are caught violating the curfew to buy food for their families so they don't starve, the police lock them in dog cages and cart them up and down the streets to shame them publicly while the drug war continues to take countless lives.

Enzo's parents raised him to care about others, to care about the world, to try to make it better. They taught him to admire the heroes of their homelands who fought the good fight. But how can anyone truly feel all this suffering and not want to give up? He can't do anything about any of it. He can't even get his dad and his lolo to have a single conversation together.

Enzo's appetite withers. His responses shrink to single syllables. He stops submitting his online schoolwork and cancels therapy sessions without telling his parents. When Kyle finally starts reaching out again, Enzo leaves his friend's texts on read. When Julia asks if he wants to talk about what's going on, he tells her no. When Chris asks if he wants to continue their rewatch of *Avatar: The Last Airbender*, Enzo shakes his head.

Instead he spends most of his time cocooned in blankets on the couch next to Thor, doomscrolling on his phone as he plays a chill video game that no longer chills him out or binge-watches problematic TV comedies from the nineties that no longer make him laugh.

Some wounds, Enzo concludes, are too deep to heal.

CHRIS

November 1983
Denver, CO

BETTER LATE THAN NEVER

The last day of school before Thanksgiving break, Chris lingers after history class and turns in his finished project to Ms. Pérez. It's twelve handwritten pages followed by four pages of perfectly cited sources.

"Wow," she says, flipping through the carefully stapled papers. "You know you only had to write three pages using four sources?"

"Yeah," Chris says, "I got a little carried away."

"The past has that power." She sets the essay down on her desk and smiles at Chris. "I started college as a mechanical engineering major. Then I took one history course as an elective, and now here I am."

Chris laughs because he gets what's she's saying in a way he wouldn't have before. Working so intensely on this project has made him regard the world with a new curiosity. When he looks around his neighborhood, he now wonders what came before the rows of homes and driveways, before the families and their sedans, before the dog walkers and joggers and lawn mowers. And when he considers the people around him, he wonders about everything that brought them into existence, everything that made them what they are—for better or worse.

He has come to appreciate the way history is not the memorization of facts, but rather a way of seeing. A way of looking at the world and understanding how the past acts as an invisible force perpetually shaping the present.

But he doesn't yet know how to articulate this shift of perspective, so instead he just says, "Thanks for letting me turn it in even though it was due, like, forever ago."

"Better late than never," says Ms. Pérez.

"Wish all my teachers believed that. And, um, thanks for actually giving us an interesting assignment."

She laughs. "You're welcome? Assuming that was a compliment."

"It was," he clarifies. "Plus it helped me forget about football."

Chris moves to leave, but Ms. Pérez asks, "What did your dad think about it?"

"About my paper?"

She nods.

"He hasn't read it."

"Why not?"

Chris's mind replays all the times he tried to share what he'd learned with his dad, their conversation in the car that night after he watched the tape with the news segment about Ninoy Aquino's assassination. "He's not that interested in the past."

"But given your topic, you must have had some fascinating conversations with him while you were doing your research."

Chris lets out a sarcastic laugh. "We don't really have 'conversations.'"

"That's too bad."

"I guess."

"After I get the paper back to you, maybe you can give it to him. Who knows, maybe it'll give the two of you something to talk about. A starting point. 'Better late than never' applies to more than just school assignments."

"I'll think about it." Chris shrugs, shifts his weight from one foot to the other. "I've got to get going, though. Thanks again, Ms. Pérez."

"And thank *you* for taking the assignment seriously, Mr. Maghabol," she says, pronouncing his last name accurately.

"Have a good Thanksgiving."

"You too," she says. "But once you dig into the history of this holiday, you may find that's not such an easy thing to do anymore."

Chris considers this. "So sometimes it's better not to know?"

"Never," Ms. Pérez says, shaking her head. "It's facing the truth—even when it's difficult—that allows us to change for the better."

A REAL FATHER

One night, back when Chris was eleven, he couldn't sleep, so he went downstairs to grab a snack and watch some TV with the volume turned down. But as he was walking down the steps, he heard his parents arguing in low voices in the kitchen. He stopped short, sat on the landing just out of sight, and listened.

"Emil, please be reasonable," came his mom's voice.

"I am being reasonable, Linda," his dad said. "There's no point in going. He barely ever spoke to us."

"He was your father."

"Ha. That man wasn't a father to me."

"I know you're still working through a lot of issues around that, but—"

"There's nothing to work through," Emil said. "It's simple."

"Is it, though?"

Silence.

Linda went on. "Getting some closure might be good for you. And if nothing else, it could be an opportunity for the kids to meet your family, to learn more about their grandfather."

"If he wasn't a father to me, he was less than a grandfather to them. Why should they miss a week of school to bury some stranger? What good will it do them to learn about a man who only ever called them once a year?"

"To be fair, that's not exactly his fault."

There was a pause.

"What do you mean by that?" Emil asked, voice like a growl.

"What do I mean? You always made it very clear that you didn't want him in our lives. He was only respecting your wishes."

"If he cared, he would have at least tried."

"No issues to work through, huh?"

"I don't appreciate your sarcasm, Linda."

The refrigerator hummed. The radiator clanged. Outside, snow fell slowly in the darkness.

"What about Beatriz?" Chris's mom asked.

"What about her?"

"Don't you want to be there for your mother?"

"She has my stepfather. She'll be fine."

More silence.

"I know you're not the emotional type, Emil, but are you really this cold? Do you really feel so little for the man?"

There was another beat of silence. A chair scraping across the floor. Footsteps. The soft clink of a dish being set into the sink.

Linda spoke once more, her voice laced with finality. "If the kids want to go to the funeral, I'm taking them. If you want, you can come with us. If not, then don't forget to feed the fish while we're gone."

Chris considered scurrying back to his room but decided to stay. After all, he was eleven now. He no longer needed to pretend that he was unaware of his parents' issues.

His mom paused at the bottom of the stairs, noticing him on the landing. She sighed, one hand on the banister, the other on her hip. Her expression softened. "Trouble sleeping again?"

Chris nodded.

"How much of that did you hear, baby?"

He shrugged.

"So. What do you think? Want to go to California for your grandfather's funeral?"

Chris hesitated. He was curious about his late grandfather, of course, but he didn't want to make his dad even angrier than he already was.

Emil appeared at the bottom of the steps, met Chris's eyes, and held his gaze until Chris looked down.

"No," Chris said. "It's okay."

"Are you sure?"

He nodded.

Linda sighed. "Okay, then. Your choice. I'll ask your sisters in the morning." She continued upstairs, tousling his shaggy black hair as she passed. "Make sure to get some sleep."

Chris's dad gave him a small nod, made his way up to the landing, sat next to Chris, and said nothing for a long time.

"I want what's best for you and your sisters," Emil said when he finally spoke. "I make sure the only thing you need to worry about is school so you can focus on your education and make the most of the opportunities afforded to you. That is what a real father does." He paused. Sighed. Went on. "My father was not like that. He cared more about other people— people he didn't even know—than he ever cared about his real family. As a result, I had to work every minute I was not in school. After my shift, I did my homework on the windowsill by the light of the streetlamps because he wouldn't let me turn on the lights in our apartment. If I hadn't worked so much, then we wouldn't have had enough to eat. If I hadn't done my homework, then I wouldn't have been smart enough to go to college. Do you understand, Christopher?"

Chris nodded.

"He was never a real father," Emil said.

A familiar silence settled between them, a fog so thick they couldn't see each other. Chris didn't know what to say to this. What child knows how to navigate the unmapped terrain of their parent's grief?

It turned out Chris didn't have to say anything, though. His dad stood up a moment later, gave Chris's shoulder a reassuring squeeze, then disappeared.

It would also turn out that neither Amy nor Jenny wanted to go to the funeral of a man they only knew as a scratchy voice at the end of a long-distance call on their birthdays.

So none of them traveled to California. None of them grieved with family and community. None of them listened to the eulogies and learned of his life. None of them watched the burial.

How many of our ancestors have returned to the earth in such a silent way?

Impervious to Good Sense

It's late when the Maghabols return from spending the day with Linda's family in Colorado Springs as they do every Thanksgiving. Emil idles the van in the driveway as Chris climbs out into the freezing cold and opens the garage door. After Emil pulls in and kills the engine, everyone else ambles out, stuffed from a day spent eating mashed potatoes, a turkey his uncle had himself hunted, and a dozen other dishes.

"Can I go over to Hazel's?" Chris asks his parents as his sisters head straight inside.

"No," Emil says.

"Sure, honey," Linda says.

Chris's parents exchange a tense look.

"Will her parents be home?" Emil asks.

"Yeah," Chris says.

"Yeah?"

"Yes. Her parents shall be present in their residence."

"One hour," Emil decides.

"Two," Linda amends.

Emil lets out an exasperated sigh. "Don't forget, you need to be up early."

"I know," Chris says. "The lights."

"Have fun," Linda says, and kisses him on the cheek.

Mounds of plowed and shoveled snow line the way to Hazel's house, and the below-freezing air stings the inside of Chris's nostrils as he tries his best not to slip on the icy sidewalks. Thankfully Hazel only lives a couple of streets away.

Mr. Young answers the door, his face breaking into a wide smile. "If it isn't Tony Dorsett himself."

"Um," Chris says.

"Oh, sorry—that's right, you stopped playing. Probably for the best. We'll find a better nickname for you yet. Doubt that's why you're here, though." He winks.

"Hazel's not asleep yet, is she?" Chris asks, pretending he didn't notice the wink because it's not like that between him and Hazel.

"Nope. She's out back with her friend."

"Which friend?" he asks, as if that's the confusing part of the statement rather than the fact that they're hanging out outside at night when it must be, like, ten degrees.

"That girl from the Philippines. You know her, don't you?"

"Becs?"

"Yeah, that's her." Mr. Young gestures for Chris to go ahead and join them, so Chris thanks him and makes his way around to the backyard.

He doesn't see anyone in the darkness at first, as the lawn chairs on the back patio where he expects to find Hazel and Becs are empty. But then he spots the two girls lying together on the trampoline under several blankets. Kissing.

"Oh!" Chris says aloud before he can stop himself.

The girls scramble apart, and Becs buries her face in the blankets while Hazel whips around.

"Oh—it's just you," she says, relieved. Then to Becs, "It's okay. It's just Chris." Then to Chris again, "It *is* okay, right?"

"You don't need my permission," he says.

Becs sits up, laughing as she covers her face with her hands. "Hi, Chris."

"Hi, Becs," he says, laughing with her. Sure, he's surprised. But only because Hazel came out to him years ago and has never actually been with anyone. If he's learned anything from his dad's unrelenting attempts to control his life, it's the importance of letting people be who they are.

"What are you doing sneaking up on us like that, you little perv?" Hazel asks. "Nearly gave me a fucking heart attack. I thought you were my dad, for Christ's sake."

"You think he'd have a problem with it?"

"I'm not ready to find out."

"Fair enough." He turns to go. "I'll let you two get back to it."

"Now that you've gone and ruined our moment, you may as well stay and hang out. Right, Becs?"

"Sure," Becs says. "Why not?"

Chris turns around and makes his way over to the trampoline.

"So," Hazel says. "Any particular reason you stopped by?"

"I finished that history paper."

"Finally," Hazel says. "But something tells me you didn't drag your ass over here in the freezing cold for a gold star."

"Ms. Pérez thinks I should let my dad read it after she gets it back to me."

"And what do you think?"

Chris isn't sure if he wants to get into all that in front of Becs. But then he remembers how he already told her all about him and his dad. "That he won't care."

"Okay, then don't."

"But—"

"But you want him to care, don't you?" Hazel says as if springing a trap. "Admit it!"

Chris hesitates. Nods.

"Then you already know what you should do."

Chris hesitates. Nods.

Hazel pushes all the covers onto Becs and stands. "Now that that's settled, I'm going to pop back inside and grab a couple more blankets."

"And some hot chocolate?" Becs pleads.

Hazel walks off the trampoline, bouncing a bit with each step. "With the little marshmallows?"

"With the little marshmallows," Becs confirms.

"I'll take a mug, too, please," Chris says.

"Be right back." Hazel heads inside the house.

Becs crawls over to the side of the trampoline and sits so her legs are dangling over the edge. Chris readjusts his beanie and digs his hands even deeper into his coat pockets, not sure what to say. "So . . . did you spend Thanksgiving here?"

"Yeah," Becs says. "My family wasn't planning to do anything since we don't celebrate it in the Philippines. But Hazel wanted me to experience it."

"And was it everything you dreamed it would be?"

"The turkey was kind of dry. The macaroni and cheese was delicious. We watched an entire football game, but I still don't understand any of the rules. How was yours?"

"Hung out with my mom's side of the family. Not the most fun in the world. But not terrible. Only thing that really sucked was that nobody told them I had to quit football, so I had to explain all of that again."

"Yikes," Becs says.

Chris nods. A few awkward seconds pass. "So . . . you and Hazel . . . how long have you been together?"

"Only a couple weeks," she says. "It's still pretty new."

"She's a good person," Chris says. "Like, one of the best I know."

"Same."

"Don't break her heart."

"I'll try my best not to."

Chris nods. Looks up. The sky is full of stars sharpened by the cold. "So that paper I was talking to Hazel about," he says after a few moments. "I wrote it about Marcos."

Becs looks up too. "Yeah, Hazel already told me. Are you expecting me to congratulate you?"

"No. I just . . . I think I have a much better idea of why your family might have moved away than I did when you first told me that was the reason."

Becs sighs. Lowers her gaze to the ground. "My tita was an activist."

"Was?"

She nods but doesn't say anything else about her aunt. And though Chris is curious about the specifics, Becs is a person, not another research project. If she wants to tell him more someday, she will.

"I have a copy of this movie that's really hard to find," Becs says after a few moments. "*Sakada*. Marcos banned it pretty much right after it came out and tried to have all the copies confiscated and destroyed."

"How'd you get it?"

"If I told you, I'd have to kill you."

Chris isn't sure if this is a joke.

"It's a joke," Becs says. "It's a bootleg recording. Not the best quality and no subtitles. I know you're finished with your project, but if you're interested, you can come over sometime and watch it. I can translate for you."

"That'd be great," Chris says.

"For a fee, of course."

"Of course."

The back door opens, spilling a slice of light across the darkness. Hazel and her dad walk out, steaming mugs of hot chocolate in hand and extra blankets over their shoulders. They set the three mugs down on the patio table as Becs and Chris walk over.

Mr. Young passes out the blankets, handing a couple to each girl and one to Chris. "You sure you kids don't want to hang out inside? I don't want to come back out later to find three giant icicles."

"We're good, Dad," Hazel says as they sit down in the patio chairs and drape the blankets over themselves.

"Ah, to be young and impervious to good sense," Mr. Young says, then heads back into the house, taking the light when he closes the door. Chris, Becs, and Hazel lift their mugs, enjoying the scent of the hot cocoa and the warmth radiating through their gloves. The girls take their first sips, but Chris starts to laugh to himself.

"Care to share with the rest of the class, Mr. Maghabol?" Hazel asks.

"Nothing," Chris says. "I was just trying to imagine *my* dad bringing us hot cocoa and blankets."

"That would be the day," Hazel says, smiling.

"He would have demanded we go inside."

"And you would have said nothing and refused to move. Even if it meant frostbite."

Chris nods. "You know me too well."

"Unfortunately." Hazel smirks. Becs laughs. Chris smiles as he shakes his head and then takes a sip of his hot chocolate—which burns his tongue.

Becs starts telling Hazel about what Christmastime is like in the Philippines, and the conversation moves on. Chris is only half listening. His brain lingers on Hazel's frostbite joke, which reminds him of Becs's comments that day in the library. It's true that his rebellion against Emil often takes the form of silent self-sabotage. But he's starting to imagine what it might mean to truly stand up for himself, to truly speak. Maybe that starts with letting his dad read his writing to see what he has to say.

ALL THERE IS TO KNOW

The next morning Chris sits on the roof, holding a spiky coil of freshly untangled Christmas lights. The snowcapped Rockies loom at his back. The sun rises in his eyes. It's still cold as hell, but Chris keeps quiet because the last time he complained about the temperature, Emil had simply said, *If you feel cold, that means you failed to dress appropriately.* The morning after Thanksgiving they put up the lights. That's what they do.

It's Chris's job to feed the lights to Emil, who stands atop the ladder and hangs the cords on the hooks he installed in the fascia the year they moved in. As Emil works his way across the house, Chris follows, scooting along the roof. It's an efficient system, refined over the years, that eliminates the riskiest parts of the task for either of them—so long as the shingles aren't frosted with ice.

They usually complete the job in silence, but when Emil climbs the ladder and stretches out his gloved hand for the next segment of lights, Chris says, "So . . . I turned in that history paper a few days ago."

"What history paper?" Emil asks.

Chris passes his dad a section of the multicolored lights, trying to stifle his annoyance. "The one I've been working on at the library. The ancestral history one."

"Oh," Emil says, wrapping the cord once around each hook. "About time."

Chris scoots along the roof. Hands over the next portion. Waits for his dad to ask to read the paper.

Emil does not ask.

"It was actually a really interesting project," Chris adds as they keep working.

"Yes, I know. . . . You wouldn't stop talking about it."

Chris tightens his grip on the lights.

Emil goes on. "I still can't believe your teacher let you choose Marcos as a topic."

"Why wouldn't she?"

"You're not Filipino," he says, then climbs down before Chris can respond.

Chris's anger simmers as he waits for Emil to get to the ground, move the ladder, and climb back up. By the time he does, Chris has managed to calm himself a bit by taking a few deep breaths.

"I am Filipino," Chris says, forcing the conversation to restart. "I mean, we are. Filipino American. But still Filipino. So it's good to learn about the Philippines, right? Like, what happens over there affects us over here. And what happens over here affects them over there."

Emil keeps working. "Nonsense."

"It's not nonsense, Dad."

"You spend a few weeks in the library and suddenly you know everything?"

Chris thinks of all the books and articles and testimonies he read. All the photos he examined. All the documentaries and news segments he watched. He thinks of Becs's aunt. "I don't know everything," he says. "But I know more than you."

Emil stops cold. Glares up at Chris. "You do, do you?"

"About Marcos, I mean."

"Uh-huh."

Chris's mouth goes dry. "Maybe you can read my paper, and—"

"Let me stop you there, Christopher." Emil rubs his forehead. "I don't need to read your paper. *I've* been alive longer than the man's been president, and I watch the news every evening. I know enough."

"But, Dad—"

"Frankly, I'll be surprised if you even get a passing grade. All those bits of trivia you've been spouting sound like Communist propaganda. If you found truly reliable, objective sources, you should also have learned about the positive things the man's done for that country."

"Like what?"

"Like . . ." Emil scoffs. "I don't know. A lot. And he's friends with President Reagan, isn't he?"

"So what if he's friends with Reagan?"

"Then that means he must be a pretty good leader."

Chris has no idea how to respond to this.

Emil sighs. Motions for Chris to continue handing him the lights. "It sounds like you put a lot of work into this project."

"I did," Chris says, glad that his dad is at the very least conceding this.

But then Emil finishes his thought. "Work that could have been better spent completing all of your other assignments."

Chris's shoulders tense. He takes another slow, deep breath. "I thought the whole reason you made me quit the team and go to the library every day is because you wanted me to focus more on school."

"Yes, that's right."

"And I have been. So what's the problem?"

Emil shifts his attention from the lights to Chris, glaring again. "Watch the attitude, Christopher."

Chris doesn't look away, doesn't let his dad shut him down. "It's just a question."

Emil shakes his head, descends, moves the ladder, climbs back up. They're nearly finished now.

"I'm glad you finally turned it in," Emil goes on. "But imagine if you took all the time and energy you wasted on that little project and put it toward classes that would actually be useful to you in the future."

"Like math or science?" Chris asks, voice flat.

"Exactly," Emil says, missing the sarcasm.

"I'm not you."

"That's clear enough."

Emil holds out a hand, but Chris passes nothing. "God, Dad, why are you like this? It wasn't a waste of time to me. I'm really interested in this stuff, and I think it's important. Maybe I'll even major in history when I go to college."

"College—with your grades?"

"Yes, with my grades."

"Unless you seriously start putting in some effort, no decent college is going to accept you. And if by some long shot that does happen, you better believe I won't be paying for you to get some useless degree."

"I don't need your help."

"That'll be the day."

Chris clenches his jaw, stares out over the neighborhood, eyes hot with tears barely held back. How he wishes the day would reset so he could keep his trap shut and never bring up the paper.

Emil slowly blinks, sighs, and softens his voice. "Why are you getting so upset over this? It was just a history assignment, Christopher."

"It's not just some assignment, Dad. It's that you never bothered teaching me anything about our people's history, about where we came from, because you didn't think it was important. Well, I do. And now I have to teach myself everything."

"It isn't important. You'll understand that when you're older."

"You couldn't even be bothered to teach us Tagalog."

"You're not some FOB, Christopher. You're a third-generation American, for crying out loud. And besides, our family wasn't even Tagalog—they were Ilokano."

"Whose fault is it that I don't know that?"

Emil shakes his head. "I've done everything I can to teach you how to be successful in this world, and that's what's important. If you've failed to learn that lesson, it's your fault alone. So go ahead, waste your life reading old books and memorizing facts nobody cares about. Just don't come crying to me when you fail to find a job that earns enough money to take care of your family."

Chris opens his mouth to argue—but then wavers. Bites his tongue. It would be a waste of words. He shuts the furnace door on the fire smoldering in his chest, submits to the silence. Wordlessly, they finish the job and climb down.

Emil plugs the cord into the power strip—but the lights stay unlit.

He curses under his breath. "We're going to have to test every bulb."

Chris removes his gloves and drops them on the driveway. "Do it yourself." Then he turns and starts for Hazel's house.

"Where do you think you're going, young man?"

Chris doesn't answer. He doesn't turn around.

"You better get back here, or else—"

Chris keeps walking.

Because Emil will never listen, never understand. People like him live their life in a fog, devoid of curiosity and context, isolated and deluded by the false belief that they already know all there is to know about everything, everyone.

Chris vows to never be a man like that. A father like that. If he ever has children, he will not force them to live some narrow life defined by narrow-minded ideas. He will make sure they know where they come from so that they can be whoever they are, so that they can become whoever they want to become.

And he will love the hell out of them no matter what.

EMIL

September 1965
Stockton, CA

To Delano

Buses idle at the curb of the station as downtown Stockton begins to stir. Passengers wait to board, still shuttered into themselves. They carry duffel bags slung across their shoulders or stand with suitcases at their feet. They clear throats, turn pages, or huddle together in whispered conversation with those who will see them off. It is the subdued air of a liminal space, the look before the leap.

Emil's dreams are still dissolving when the white driver walks past and climbs into the bus, starts the engine, and calls for Delano-bound passengers. Emil pushes off the wall he's been leaning against, joins the short line, stomps up the steps, and slides into an open seat near the back. The vinyl cushion is stiff, the window damp from the humidity. Emil wipes it with the bottom of his fist and gazes at the sky lightening behind the downtown buildings. Through the moisture-smeared glass, the sight of his waking city already makes him feel distant and alone. He is an astronaut orbiting Earth, overcome with the sense he will never again step foot on its soil. Is this what Francisco feels each time he leaves?

Before Leon's threat, Emil had made up his mind to simply spend the day observing Francisco and his people's work, keeping his mind open to the possibility that a good education might make him an ally instead of an adversary, without promising anything. But now he doesn't know what he's going to say to his father once he arrives—or what he'll do once he returns.

He could carry on as planned, say nothing to his father, and start searching for new employment tomorrow. However, jobs for Filipinos—jobs not in the fields—are hard to come by in Stockton. Who knows how long it would take, how long his mother would be without his wages?

The other option: try to convince his father to quit unionizing.

If Emil asks, though, Francisco will definitely refuse, and whatever remaining respect Francisco holds for Emil will irrevocably vanish. The man puts nothing before the movement. Emil's childhood was a constellation of conflicts between his parents around this exact issue. The last time Emil's mother had a miscarriage, Francisco was away organizing and didn't even cut his trip short after receiving the news.

Still, if Emil can say he honestly tried, maybe Auntie Carmen will let him continue working at the café.

As Emil considers the lose-lose situation awaiting him in Delano, the bus driver leans out the door and makes a final call for passengers. Someone shouts for him to wait.

Emil peers out the window and sits up. It's his classmate Sammy Bautista in a denim jacket with a fleece-lined collar, carrying an expensive-looking camera around his neck and a duffel bag over his shoulder. He hands his ticket to the driver, boards, and scans the bus for a place to sit.

Before Emil can anguish over how to react, Sammy spots him, smiles, and makes his way over. "If it isn't Emilio Maghabol!" He raises an eyebrow. "May I?"

Emil shifts to make sure he's not crossing the imaginary boundary between the seats. "Um, sure, Sammy."

"Salamat, pare!" Sammy hoists his bag up onto the overhead luggage rack and drops himself down next to Emil. "On your way to Delano, ha?"

Emil nods, noticing the scent of mint that arrives with Sammy. His aftershave, probably.

"Right on," Sammy says.

"Sure."

Sammy gets himself situated as the bus pulls out of the station. "I suppose you're joining your father on the front lines."

"Something like that," Emil says, tucking away the newspaper he'd been planning to read. "You know my father's there?"

Sammy laughs. "Of course—show me a self-respecting Pinoy on the West Coast who doesn't!"

The same awe glimmers in Sammy's voice that shone in the eyes of those listening to his father's speech that night in their apartment. Annoyingly, Emil feels a pang of pride again.

"He certainly keeps busy," Emil says. "So why are you going to Delano?"

Sammy holds up his camera.

"A camera."

Sammy lowers his camera. "Very good, Emilio Maghabol. No wonder you finished the year at the top of your class."

"You can call me Emil."

Sammy smiles. "Okay, Emil Maghabol."

"I meant just Emil."

"Okay, Just Emil."

It's a corny joke, but Emil's laugh is genuine. "Shouldn't you be headed to somewhere like Big Sur or Yosemite instead? Somewhere real beautiful, you know? Nothing's in Delano."

"Our people are in Delano. And they're beautiful, don't you think?"

Emil shrugs. Looks down. "I don't know. Some of them, I suppose."

"Well, I think they all are. But the main reason I'm going down there is to document this strike your father's helping to organize."

"Why?"

"It's gonna be important—we'll need to remember it."

"You really think so?"

"I do, Just Emil."

Emil wants to ask why, but as the only son of the great Francisco Maghabol, he's supposed to already know the answer to that question. Instead he nods.

As the bus glides along the highway, their conversation turns away from the impending grape strike and toward life in general. They talk about books and movies, finding they have surprisingly similar tastes. They tell funny stories about their families and their teachers and their classmates. They commiserate about the racism they've both faced everywhere in Stockton outside Little Manila. Sammy shares his plan to double major in history and political science at Berkeley after he graduates. Emil talks about wanting to find a career that involves mathematics.

The hours fly by, and soon the vineyards of the Central Valley are rolling past, rows peppered with field laborers stooping over the crops in direct sunlight.

"We're almost there." Sammy points his camera out the window, and the shutter clicks several times.

"Guess so," Emil says, trying to see what Sammy sees.

They're soon greeted by a WELCOME TO DELANO! sign on the side of the road. Houses and cement buildings gradually replace the hills and fields.

Panic takes root in Emil's gut as he realizes he still does not know what he's going to do about his father. He starts to open his mouth to tell Sammy about the situation, to ask for his advice. But then he closes it. He doesn't want to correct the vision Sammy must have of Emil heading off to fight the good fight by his father's side.

The bus pulls into the station. The driver kills the engine. Sammy grabs his bag and then shoots Emil a quizzical glance when he notices that Emil carries only a folded newspaper. "You sure are traveling light."

"Yeah," Emil says with a chuckle but offers no additional explanation.

They shuffle down the aisle and off the bus, into an open sky and an oppressive early-afternoon heat. Sammy hands his camera to a random woman and asks her to take a picture of him and Emil. She takes the picture, hands the camera back.

"I'm headed this way," Sammy says, gesturing to the south. "You?"

"Wherever the Filipino Hall is."

Sammy points his camera north. "It's only a few blocks that way." Then he takes out a pen, scribbles something on a scrap of paper, and gives it to Emil. It's a phone number. "My uncle's apartment. I'll be staying there for the next few weeks."

"Oh."

"But I'm sure we'll cross paths on the picket line."

"Right," Emil says, giving Sammy nothing.

They shake hands and say goodbye. Then Emil sets off to locate his father, hoping to find the right words before he finds the man.

A COUNTRY OF BROKEN
PROMISES

The sun beats down on the squat stucco building of the Filipino Hall, which is, as Sammy assured him, only a short walk from the bus station. Most everyone will still be out in the fields since it's the middle of the day, but this is where Francisco had told Emil to meet him.

Emil wipes the sweat from his brow and the back of his neck with a handkerchief, then walks up the short flight of steps to the entrance, still unsure of what to do about his father. He tries the door, finds it unlocked, and steps inside.

Cool air hits, carrying a mildewy scent. It's a small square space dimly lit, curtains drawn to keep out the sun. It's flimsy folding chairs clustered around collapsible tables, stacks of extras in the corner. It's fake tile floors. It's off-white walls crowded with framed photographs, Philippine and American flags, union crests, community organization banners, and patches bearing the emblems of the First and Second Filipino Infantry Regiments as well as the ships those in the Navy had served on during WWII. It's large dark-green painted words above a short bandstand that proclaim, FILIPINO COMMUNITY OF DELANO. It's decades of weddings, meetings, banquets, debuts, dances, parties, potlucks.

Emil calls out a few times, but there's no response. He checks his watch, and his usual frustration with Francisco flares up. He had hoped his father would be here himself, but he at least expected the presence of someone from the union. Now he might have to waste the day searching for his father, allowing his anxiety and indecision to continue simmering.

Emil decides to wait at least half an hour before stepping back into the sun. He considers reading but instead decides to examine the walls. As he takes in the faded faces, he remembers what Sammy Bautista said about all their people being beautiful. Sammy, no doubt, would appreciate the history that permeates this space. He would regard it as sacred instead of mundane and would probably be taking pictures of the pictures or maybe of Emil looking at them.

A woman appears, startling Emil. She's an older dark-skinned Filipina stirring a cup of instant coffee with wrinkled hands. "Good afternoon po," Emil greets.

She holds out her hand, and he presses the back of it to his forehead for the mano po blessing.

"I'm looking for my father," he continues. "Francisco Maghabol. Mang Isko, people call him. Do you know where I might find him?"

"Ah, Isko! You must be his oldest son, ha?" the woman says in Ilokano. "Just as handsome."

"His only son," Emil says, sticking to English. "Do you know where he is?"

The woman pushes the cup of coffee into his hands and shepherds him onto a chair at one of the small tables. She disappears into the back and returns a few minutes later bearing a flimsy paper plate loaded with garlic rice, beef tapa, a fried egg, and pandesal. After setting the food down in front of Emil like an offering, she sits next to him.

"Thank you, but, um," Emil says, "my father—"

"I'm Lola Mar."

"Nice to meet you, Lola. I'm Emil, but—"

"Emil," she repeats. "Emilio. Like General Aguinaldo."

"Sure."

Lola Mar smiles and nods. Gestures for him to eat.

Emil would much rather have some cereal and toast than these room-temperature leftovers, but he hasn't eaten anything all day, so he picks up the fork and spoon and digs in.

"If you came here for work, this is not a good time," she says.

"I didn't—like I said, I'm looking for my father, Francisco. Can you tell—"

"They're going to strike soon, so there will be many jobs. But if you take a job, then you'll be betraying your countrymen. You're not a traitor, are you?"

Great. She's one of them. Emil checks his watch. "I'm not here for a job, Lola. I'm here to—"

"This is a strange country, yes?" she interrupts.

"I don't know." He dips his pandesal in the egg yolk and takes a bite.

"My whole family, we fight for the United States in the Philippines during the war. Me, my husband, Cresente, and our three boys. We are part of the guerilla forces. They tell the Filipinos, 'These islands are American territory. If you defend them, we will pay you. After we defeat the Japanese, you can become American. You can move to America. You can take your family. You will get benefits. We will take care of you for the rest of your life.'"

Emil doesn't want to hear this woman's entire life story, but then he thinks about what Sammy would do. Instead of interrupting her to ask after his father again, he resigns himself to listening.

Lola Mar continues. "We hide in the mountains, and we fight. The Americans run away, but we keep fighting without them because we are fighting for our home. We bury many friends. We bury one son. Then a second. Then our last. Every night it feels like we will be the next ones in the ground. We even begin to pray for it. But then we defeat the Japanese. The Americans return just before the very end and say it is because of them we win. They allow some of us to go to America. Me and Cresente go because our children are dead and we have nothing else left. But then after we are already here, do you know what the Americans do?"

"What?" Emil asks, genuinely interested.

"They say, 'The Philippines is now independent, so we will not make you citizens unless you were already living here before the war. And because you are not citizens, we will not pay you or give you benefits for fighting the Japanese. Instead we will give money to your government'—as if the Americans had not claimed to be our government during the war—'then we will let them distribute it.' Of course, our government does not distribute anything to those of us who are already gone."

Emil listens. He didn't know any of this. It sounds like the kind of thing his father would rant about. Maybe he had and Emil just hadn't paid attention. "After all that, they really gave you nothing, Lola?" he asks.

The old woman sighs. "They tell us that it is more than enough to let us come here. That this is the land of opportunity. That if we work hard and obey the law, we can become richer than we ever would have back home. But when we come here, nobody wants to hire us for anything. Back home I was a nurse, and Cresente was a teacher. Here no hospital will hire me, and no school will hire him. So we work in the fields. We try to save, but they are not paying us very much. One day Cresente dies because he is working too hard. Then it is only me working in the fields. Only me alone in this country. Only me."

She falls quiet. Takes a sip of coffee. Emil expects her to cry given the depth of the loss she just shared, but she doesn't. Perhaps it's been too many years. Perhaps she's told this story too many times.

"I'm sorry that happened to you," he says. "That's not fair." And he means it. It's not right for the government to say one thing and do another, especially when that altered the entire course of this woman's life.

"This is a country of broken promises," she says. "They would have us believe that we were the ones to fail, that it is our fault alone if we do not have the lives we want. That it is our fault we are still toiling in the fields after all these years." She pauses. Rests her hand on his. "So I am thankful for angels like your father who continue to fight for our dignity, our lives, when everyone else would sooner forget we still exist."

Emil leans back, pulling his hand away in shame at how often he's mentally disparaged his father's efforts.

But Lola Mar reaches out and touches Emil's face. She smiles. "You look like my youngest." Then she pushes herself to her feet and leaves without saying anything else.

Emil considers going after her but figures she didn't answer his questions about Francisco because she doesn't know where he is. Instead he finishes the rest of his food and coffee while turning her story over in his mind, unsettled.

His white teachers and Auntie Carmen always blamed the struggles of the farmworkers on their lack of work ethic or intelligence, their refusal to assimilate, their insistence on stirring up trouble. But Lola Mar's life doesn't fit that narrative. It's not her fault the United States refused to grant her or her husband citizenship after promising to do so. It's not her fault she ended up having to work in the fields after nobody would hire her as a nurse simply because she was Filipina.

How many others have stories like this? If so, then what? Shouldn't that matter?

Emil is certain he cannot find out the answers to these questions by the time the midnight bus departs, but for the first time, he wants to.

Maybe he will stay a bit longer.

CONTINENTAL DIVIDE

After a few hours asking around town in the overwhelming heat, Emil still cannot find his father. Person after person tells him that Francisco always turns up at the Filipino Hall, so as the sun dips low in the sky, Emil resigns himself to return and wait.

There's a group of old-timers playing cards around a table. They're arguing loudly but stop when they notice Emil enter. One of them—a short, stocky man with a cowboy hat, a patchy gray beard, and arms corded with muscle from a life spent clearing and planting and cutting and harvesting—welcomes Emil in Visayan. Emil returns the greeting in English.

"Here for the meeting?" the man asks, switching over to English as he waves Emil over.

"Maybe," Emil says. "I'm looking for my father. Francisco Maghabol?"

"Ah yes, Isko. Of course. A good man. I'm Celestino."

"Emil." They shake. Then Emil goes around the table shaking the other men's hands. After the introductions are complete, Celestino drags over a chair for Emil.

"Thank you, Manong," Emil says as he joins them. "Do you know if my father will be at this meeting?"

"Sure, sure," Celestino says as he shuffles the deck of cards. "He'll probably come with Larry, Phil, Andy, and Pete."

"What time is it supposed to start?" Emil asks.

"Seven."

Emil checks his watch. It's just past four.

"Shall I deal you in?" Celestino asks. "You speak English like you've got money to spare."

Knowing how Filipinos operate, seven will probably be closer to eight thirty or nine, so Emil says, "Sure."

Celestino continues shuffling. "This is your first time in here, ha?"

"I actually came by a few hours ago."

"How'd you get in?" one of the other old-timers asks. "We've been keeping the door locked because we can't trust the growers not to plant a bomb these days."

"Or any days," says another.

"It was open," Emil says. "An old woman was here—Lola Mar. She gave me some food, I spoke with her for a bit, then she left."

Celestino freezes. "Lola Mar? You certain, kid?"

"Yes, that was her name. I'm sure of it. She told me about her life. About fighting against the Japanese during the war and losing her sons."

"That was Lola Mar, all right." Celestino exchanges a grim look with the others and then turns back to Emil. He puts down the cards, removes his hat, and makes the sign of the cross. "But she died last year."

A chill runs down Emil's spine. "Oh, um . . ."

Celestino's face breaks into a grin, and he punches Emil playfully on the shoulder. "Nah, just pulling your leg. She's still alive. Old as hell but alive." He turns to his friends, rattles off something in Visayan, and they all laugh with him.

Emil's face flushes. He hates being the butt of the joke.

"But you say you spoke with her, ha?" Celestino asks as he puts his hat back on and continues shuffling.

Emil nods.

"So you know Ilokano?"

"I understand it, but I can't really speak it."

He smirks. "Then you probably didn't speak *with* her."

"What do you mean?"

Celestino places the cards on the table in front of Emil. "She doesn't know English, kid."

As the old-timers crack up, Emil cuts the deck, feeling stupid. However, he's better at cards than many people since he's good with numbers and spent his childhood around gamblers. He'll make them hurt a bit for laughing at him.

Emil intentionally loses the first several hands to study each man while letting them gain a false sense of confidence. And it works. Soon they're laughing and loose, overplaying their hands and revealing all their tells. Emil acts appropriately frustrated.

A few other men trickle into the community hall, setting up their own games or gathering around the table, nudging one another and spreading word that the kid losing all his money is Mang Isko's son. The audience's presence makes the other players even more confident, sloppier.

Then Emil truly begins playing.

"Finally a bit of luck," Emil says after he wins the next hand.

"Too little, too late," Celestino says.

Coin by coin, bill by bill, the winnings slide across the table to Emil, the momentum shifting like the tide. The laughter dies, and the old-timers around the table grow sullen while those observing make fun of their losses. Soon Emil has almost three times the amount he started with in a pile in front of him. Confusion gives way to anger as the other players grow suspicious that the boy has been hustling them.

Emil intentionally loses a few times to offer the men some relief, some hope. He doesn't want to push it too far. His own father once told him about the time in a Chinese gambling house in San Francisco when a desperate Filipino accused the house of cheating, drew a gun, and shot the dealer and a few others before Francisco tackled and disarmed him. Emil always doubted his father had actually been present—let alone been the hero—but it is true enough that many men do not know how to lose.

Emil makes up his mind to bow out soon, but as Celestino begins dealing the next hand, he says, "You're much better at this than your brother."

"Brother?" Emil says, cocking his head and checking his hand. It's not great. "I don't have a brother."

"Sure," Celestino says, unconvinced.

"I really don't. I'm an only child."

"I suppose you're still sore about that whole Lola-Mar-is-a-ghost joke, ha? Trying to pull *my* leg now."

Emil looks up. "I have a lot of cousins. Maybe you mean one of them?"

Celestino shakes his head. "Nope. Still not buying it. Your brother came by a couple days ago looking for Mang Isko, just like you."

A sinking feeling settles in Emil's stomach. He freezes, forgets the game, and hopes Celestino is messing with him again.

Celestino doesn't notice the change in Emil and goes on. "Isko wrapped him up in a big hug soon as he came in—saw it with my own two eyes. He even took the boy around, introducing him to everyone as his son. Proud as hell. Now, what was his name?"

"Sergio," several people answer, nearly in unison.

"Sergio. Right. Sergio from Coachella." He grins at Emil. "See, they all know, too, so you can drop the act now."

Emil is transported back to that day in the café when Auntie Gia had come back to tell Auntie Carmen that Francisco had returned from Coachella Valley. After Auntie Carmen had sent Emil to the kitchen to chop vegetables, she went back and spoke with Auntie Gia in a hushed voice. They were always gossiping, so he didn't pay it much mind. But now he wished he had.

The realization hits Emil like a brick to the back of his head.

The shock must show on his face because Celestino's eyes go wide, and he sits up straight. "Oh shit, kid—your father—you didn't know . . . Sorry."

His father has another son. Maybe even another family. Down in Coachella apparently.

All those days and weeks his father spent away—he'd been doing more than organizing workers.

Were there even more out there? Sown like seeds up and down the coast?

Celestino keeps talking, but Emil's a thousand miles away. Without saying anything, Emil folds, pockets his winnings, and leaves. In a daze, he walks down the street in the long shadows cast by the setting sun.

What a fucking hypocrite.

All Francisco's noble ideas. All his fighting for the people. All his pretending to be a hero. And for what? So he could go around screwing a bunch of women?

Had the man ever been real, been truly honest, a single day in his entire life?

Under a humming streetlight, Emil finds a phone booth. Drops a coin. Dials. Listens to the ringing. His mother picks up.

"Hello?" comes Beatriz's voice, crackling and distant.

Emil tells her.

His mother is silent for a long time. So long that Emil starts to wonder if the line cut out. But then she clears her throat. "We were going to tell you eventually, honey."

For the second time, Emil feels like he's been cracked in the skull. "You knew?"

"Yes, but—"

"You knew?" he repeats, incandescent with anger. "And you stayed?"

Beatriz starts to explain, but Emil slams the receiver back into its cradle.

Before he knows it, he is back at the bus depot.

He buys a ticket. Boards. Waits.

He is the only passenger, and that's okay. He doesn't want to talk to anyone ever again.

Eventually the bus driver, a fat white man with blond hair, rises from his seat behind the wheel and steps into the doorway. He cups his hands around his mouth and shouts to the nearly empty station, "Last call for Stockton."

He waits a few moments, returns to his place behind the wheel, and catches Emil's eye in the long overhead mirror. "Looks like it's just you, boy."

It's always been just me, Emil thinks.

The engine rumbles to life. They pull away from the curb, passing a bus bound for Denver, according to its destination sign. And then they're on the road, moving away from the station. Away from Delano and the workers preparing to strike. Away from Francisco, like cutting an anchor free.

Emil searches his soul and finds it calm as the river on a Sunday morning. He's done. Done toying with the idea of joining a false movement led by false men. Done reaching for Francisco. He will endure two more years at home, graduate, go to college somewhere far away from the family that's lied to him for who knows how long. Start a new life. Make of it what he wants, what he can. Nobody and nothing to hold him back except himself.

Emil imagines coasting across the Rockies on that Denver-bound bus someday and likes the idea of putting a mountain range between his father and himself. He wants nothing less than a continental divide.

FRANCISCO

January 1930
Watsonville, CA

Every White Man
in Watsonville

Francisco is enjoying a drink along the wall as he watches the couples dancing to the band's rendition of "After You've Gone." But he begins to notice a few people whispering to one another and then peeling away from the crowd to disappear downstairs.

A knife fight between two men wanting to dance with the same woman, perhaps. It certainly wouldn't be the first. But as the crowd continues to thin, Francisco peers out one of the windows, curious about what might be drawing everyone away. His stomach drops as he takes in the view.

Gathered under the streetlights in front of the dance hall seems to be every white man in Watsonville. They stand shoulder to shoulder, forming a thick wall spanning the length of the building, trucks parked behind them in a semicircle like a barricade. There must be at least two or three hundred, if not more. They hold clubs and staves and blackjacks and coils of rope. In their eyes, hatred and the promise of violence.

Francisco catches Lorenzo's attention across the room and waves him over. Lorenzo looks out the window and curses.

The band sputters out. The dance floor empties. An oppressive hush replaces the joy and music that had filled the space only moments before, and the sound of the ocean crashing against the shore reclaims the air.

Eventually one of the white men steps forward and raps on the door with his club. The banging reverberates through the building as he steps back, and the dance hall takes a collective breath.

The man scans the crowd of watching brown faces. "We don't want any trouble. Just let us in so we can retrieve our girls."

Francisco and the others turn to the white women among them. Their already pale faces have gone ashen. Some cling to the men they had been dancing with or to one another. Some simply clench their jaws, cross their arms, and shake their heads.

"Don't let them in," one woman says.

After a few seconds of silence, the dance hall's door opens. The two Ilokano owners step outside, shotguns raised. The white men shift as if to pounce. The man who had knocked does not move. Francisco's hands begin to tremble. His heart races, and his mouth goes dry. There's no way this will resolve peacefully.

"If you don't want any trouble," one of the owners says in English, "then leave now."

The white man with the club grins, gestures with a nod at the mob behind him. "Not without our girls."

"Nobody's forcing them to be here," the other owner says. "They're free to go whenever they want."

The man at the front of the mob calls out, "Let's go, girls."

The women do not move.

One of them—the one with the brown hair and freckles who'd told Francisco about Milly the other night—cups her hands around her mouth and yells, "Go on home, Stanley! Leave us alone!"

"They're safe with us," calls out one of the Filipino men.

The white mob mutters, like a groaning dam fit to burst.

Inside, the men debate among themselves in Ilokano, Visayan, Tagalog, and other languages.

"These motherfuckers."

"What do we do?"

"Nothing. They'll leave eventually."

"Or they'll force their way in and kill us all."

"Let them try."

"Let's send the girls out."

"That won't matter. They'll wait for us."

"They didn't care this much when we went to the dance halls *they* owned."

"We have to fight, show them we're not afraid. Or they'll keep coming back."

"We don't have any weapons."

"I have my pistol."

"I have my knife."

"I have my fists."

"Me too."

"They outnumber us as at least ten to one—we don't stand a chance."

"So what? Would you rather die like a man or a cowering rat?"

"Where are the police, ha?"

"Taking their time, no doubt."

"Some are probably down there in the mob without their uniforms."

A window shatters, a gunshot rings, people cry out in surprise or fear or anger.

In the tense beat that follows, Francisco and Lorenzo peek through the window. Smoke trails from the barrel of one of the Ilokano owner's guns, but they don't see anyone down.

In the next breath, the dam breaks, and the crowd surges forward. Another shot rings out, and chaos erupts inside the dance hall as the Filipinos and the women rush to the exits to run or to fight.

"What do we do, Manong?" Francisco asks Lorenzo as they join the crush. "Should we fight?"

"And die? No—run. If we get separated, meet back at the bunkhouse."

Eventually they spill through the doorway and into the madness. Francisco freezes at the horrible tableau unfurling under the streetlamps, the gangs of men beating his brothers. Shouts of pain, cries for help, whoops of joy, and peals of cruel laughter fill the air as wood and metal crack bone and flesh. Some fly in to fight while others scatter. Swarms of the white mob break off, engines roar to life, and trucks speed off to chase those who've escaped.

Francisco hesitates. He must help.

"There's nothing we can do, Isko," Lorenzo says as he pulls Francisco away from the chaos, toward the bluff. Francisco resists for a moment—then lets himself be pulled. They stumble and fall as they reach the beach, but there's no time to brush themselves off, so they pop up and sprint away, following the water's edge, shoes sinking into the sand with each panicked step.

THE FOURTH NIGHT

The violence lasts through the night. Some—like Francisco and Lorenzo—sneak all the way back unharmed. Others hide in rafters or crawl spaces or orchards or wherever else keeps them safe until the coast is clear. Those feared dead limp back at daybreak with fresh bruises, black eyes, bloodied noses, broken bones.

As the sun rises, they clean their wounds and consider what comes next. A few pack their things and leave town; a few, the continent. Most stay, knowing they're not wanted anywhere. The fiercer debate electrifying each bunkhouse and work camp is whether to dance again that night, certain as they are that the white mob will return if they do.

"Let's not provoke them," urges Lorenzo, who becomes the spokesperson in their bunkhouse for the side of caution. "Things will calm down and return to normal in no time."

"Then they win," someone counters.

"But we survive," Lorenzo says.

Francisco listens as the two sides argue, unsure of what to do. Lorenzo is as calm and as confident as the lawyer he'll someday surely be, but there's something simmering inside of Francisco that despises the idea of submitting to the white men's threats, no matter the danger. Who the hell are they to tell him what to do? When Francisco decides to leave this country, it will be because he chooses to, not because he's been chased away.

After the discussion in their bunkhouse dies down and everyone disperses—nobody having persuaded anyone else from their initial position—he pulls Lorenzo aside.

Having been too nervous to speak in front of the group, he now shares his opinion with his friend: "I think we should go back tonight."

Disappointment crosses Lorenzo's face. "Didn't you hear anything I said?"

"Yes, but—"

"Don't be stupid, little brother."

Francisco looks down, stung by the uncharacteristic meanness.

"Nothing's changed, right?" Lorenzo presses. "You plan to return home?"

"Sure," Francisco says.

"Well, do you want to go back to your family in a casket?"

Francisco says nothing.

"Your pride is not worth your life," Lorenzo says.

꩜

That night the defiant bathe their wounds in cold water, shine scuffed shoes, slip on torn suits, slick back frayed hair, load pistols, hide knives, then leave for the dance hall. Francisco watches with envy.

From the shameful safety of the bunkhouse, Francisco imagines the men following the trolley tracks to the dance hall. He imagines them dancing the Charleston and the foxtrot and the Texas Tommy and whatever the hell else they want to do until the band's out of breath because fuck those white folks. He imagines them laughing even more loudly, spending even more generously, and dancing with the desperation of those uncertain that they'll see the sunrise.

When they return the next morning, Francisco listens to their stories of the white boys and white men who eventually showed up at the dance hall with makeshift weapons as sharp and hard as their white-hot anger, "concerned citizens" doing their own dance. Forming a scowling wall. Shouting at the club's owners, who stood guard, and the sheriff's deputies, who—eventually—arrived armed but uncommitted. Dispersing but only to plan the evening's terrorism.

Francisco listens as they tell of how once the final song ended, they downed their last drinks and gathered their things and kissed the women good night. How they organized themselves into groups and drew their own weapons. How they took a collective breath and steeled themselves for the violence waiting in the shadows.

Francisco listens as they tell of hunting parties patrolling the town with festive glee, having a grand old time enacting this obvious solution to the Filipino question. Of those who were caught and beaten bloody or stripped naked and taunted with monkey calls or thrown over the bridge or all of the above. Of the Chinese grocer and a few other store owners who ushered fleeing Filipinos in from the street so they could hide in their rafters or back rooms while most of the town drew curtains closed and locked doors until the early morning, when the police gently dispersed the remaining "vigilantes" as if they were rambunctious children who'd gotten a bit out of hand.

"I bet it's out of their system now," Lorenzo tells Francisco.

But the next night passes in the same way.

"They'll tire themselves out," Lorenzo tells Francisco.

But then the third night passes in the same way.

"I'm sure it's over," Lorenzo tells Francisco.

But whatever has been simmering inside of Francisco reaches a boil. Lorenzo is wrong. The mob is never going to leave them alone. So when the others prepare to go out on the fourth night, he puts on a suit to join them.

"Where do you think you're going, Isko?" Lorenzo asks, his undershirt and old pair of work pants contrasting with Francisco's sharp outfit.

"Dancing."

Lorenzo scoffs. "This isn't a game—if they catch you, they'll kill you."

"Nobody's died."

"Not yet."

As soon as there's space, Francisco walks over to the shared mirror. With shaking hands, he reknots his tie. Lorenzo follows, so Francisco tells him, "You're not my tatang."

"I'm the closest thing you've got to one." Lorenzo stands next to Francisco, trying and failing to make eye contact through the mirror. "We're safe here."

"Then why have we been taking turns keeping watch?" Francisco says as he struggles to knot his tie correctly, because it's true—those who've been staying back are not completely safe either. The white mob is hungry for violence. When the chase and beatings are not enough, some have gone to the Filipinos' work camps and bunkhouses and shared apartments on lower Main Street and Pajaro to shatter windows, bust doors, and destroy whatever or whomever they can find inside until their appetites for damage are sated.

Lorenzo sighs. Shakes his head. "Don't give them a reason to go after us."

"I don't think any of us has ever done so."

"We have to prove we can be peaceful."

"We have to prove we can fight back."

"This isn't the way we fight back."

"Then what is?"

"Stay," Lorenzo says.

"I've already made up my mind—I'm going to that dance hall."

"No, I mean, if you really want to fight back, little brother, then stay. Here. In this country. Don't return to the Philippines."

"How is that fighting back?" Francisco asks.

"They want you to leave," Lorenzo says, "so stay. Survive. Get out of the fields. Go to school. Start a career. Start a family. Earn their respect and make America your home too."

Francisco smooths his lapels and shakes his head. "I'm not staying where I'm not wanted."

Lorenzo runs his hands over his face in frustration. "If you're scared, then fine, we can leave in the morning. I hear it's better up in Stockton."

"I'm not going to Stockton." Francisco puts on his hat and tilts it at an angle. "I'm going dancing."

"Just because you don't know how to read or write doesn't mean you have to be a fool, Isko."

Francisco lets out a sarcastic laugh as he turns away from the mirror to face his friend. "So. There it is. What you really think of me."

Lorenzo starts to speak, but Francisco brushes past him to join the others with fine suits and clenched fists, ready to dance.

No Going Back

It doesn't matter that Milly isn't there or that Beatriz is gone and he will probably never see either of them again or that he's gotten into an argument with his closest friend in this godforsaken country or that he might never see his family or his homeland again if the mob catches him tonight. Francisco dances and drinks and spends and smokes until he's so exhausted and so gone, he can barely stand.

Eventually, as everyone expects, the white mob arrives. They do not stay long, but their presence instantly sobers up Francisco and the other men. The band nervously plays one last song, and then everyone preps for their exit like combat veterans, having learned a few things after surviving the previous three nights.

They split into groups based on location, so Francisco goes with eight other men who live in or near his bunkhouse. One has a pistol, and three have knives. Francisco and the rest arm themselves with broken bottles. After strategizing a circuitous route back—which includes passing a handful of points where some of their countrymen will be lying in wait to help them out if need be—they kiss the women goodbye, make the sign of the cross over their hearts, and leave.

They are halfway home and far from the next checkpoint when three trucks roar up behind them and screech to a stop at their heels. Adrenaline pumping and hearts racing, Francisco and the others grip their weapons and turn. Silhouetted by the headlights, more than a dozen men hop out of the vehicles. The Filipino with the gun aims and fires—but misses—and the mob lands like a typhoon.

❧

Gradually, the hitting and kicking subside. The white men congratulate one another, laughing and out of breath. One of them spits on Francisco, who's writhing on the ground with the others. "Go back to your fucking islands, you fucking monkeys."

Footsteps fade, doors slam shut, engines start, tires kick up gravel.

Then there is the silence after the storm, the groaning of the men radiating with pain as they roll onto their sides, spit out blood or teeth, and survey the damage. Those who can push themselves back up onto their feet and help those who can't. They dust one another off and tend to one another's injuries, tearing off pieces of their own clothing to create makeshift bandages and slings.

Francisco doesn't remember how well they held their own in the fight. He doesn't even remember how long it lasted. Probably only a few minutes, even if felt like hours. But they are alive.

In fact, Francisco has never felt so alive. His heart is on fire. Finally he stood up to them. It doesn't matter that he might not have gotten in many solid hits. All that matters is that he did not spend another night cowering in the bunkhouse. He showed them that he does not fear their threats and violence.

But since having been attacked once does not mean they will not be attacked again by another group, they retreat into a nearby copse of trees to spend the rest of the night out of sight.

Francisco limps back in the morning, footsteps crunching unevenly over the layer of frost carpeting the field. His suit is rumpled and torn; the jacket, balled up under his left arm. His hat and tie and right shoe are long gone. He's got a black eye and bloodied knuckles. Too many scratches and bruises to count. Probably a broken rib or two—based on the sharp pain that accompanies every intake of breath—and a fat lip too swollen to feel the cigarette dangling from his mouth.

He reaches the bunkhouse as the sun rises over the eastern hills. It's a startlingly clear morning—no fog, no clouds—but cold as hell. After last night he's happy for any kind of morning.

"Mang Enzo!" Francisco calls as he approaches the bunkhouse. "I'm back. Those sons of bitches couldn't kill me!"

Other survivors, who have gathered outside the front of the building, pause their war stories to cheer his arrival and clap him on the back. Francisco smiles but walks past. He pulls open the creaky door, steps inside, and stops short—Lorenzo's cot is empty.

After scanning the other sleeping figures for his friend, he steps back outside. "Any of you seen Lorenzo?" he asks the gathered men.

They shake their heads and shrug, but then one says, "He went out to look for you last night."

Francisco's heart falters. His mind reels. Ignoring pain and hunger and thirst, he spits out his cigarette and heads back into the morning.

It takes a few hours, but after asking at nearly every work camp and bunk-house in the area, Francisco finally finds someone who has seen Lorenzo. The man points with his lips down the road, to the east. "He was going that way."

Francisco thanks the man and races down the road.

-ᐁ-

An old-timer leads Francisco around the side of the large building to the rear of an unfamiliar bunkhouse twice the size of where he and Lorenzo had been staying. When they turn the corner, the old man gestures toward the shadows.

"We're trying to keep him out of the sun," he explains.

At first Francisco is confused. It's a blanket laid out on the ground. But as he approaches, he makes out the shape of a body underneath. He stops. Looks up at the man.

The man nods.

Francisco's eyes return to the covered body. He doesn't move. His vision blurs. Someone clears their throat. Francisco looks up again. Others have gathered around. One strides past Francisco and pulls back the sheet.

"Skippy found him in the ditch just down the road," the man says. "Is it your friend?"

Francisco's eyes come back into focus. A body. On its back. Eyes closed. Beaten almost beyond recognition. Almost.

He can't bring himself to say yes. But it is Lorenzo—or rather, Lorenzo's body.

Slowly, Francisco drops to his knees at his friend's side. He looks up at the empty sky. A knot forms in his throat. Angry tears well in his eyes. And then something inside of him breaks. He folds himself over the body, burying his face in its bloody chest. For the first time since he crossed the ocean, he cries.

Hands rub his back, pull him up to a sitting position, lean him against the side of the bunkhouse. Someone holds him. "I'm sorry, little brother."

As Francisco holds his hands over his face, eyes shut tight against the tears, consolations come in snatches of Visayan and Ilokano and English.

"Unlucky—"

"Wrong place at the wrong time—"

"Maybe it was quick—"

"Not the only one—"

"Fermin Tobera over at Murphy Ranch also—"

"I'm sorry, little brother—"

"I'm sorry—"

"I'm sorry—"

"Be strong."

"They'll pay for this."

There are more words, but they no longer reach Francisco. It's like he's falling, bracing to hit the ground but instead keeps falling.

This is his fault.

If he hadn't insisted on joining the others at the dance hall, then Lorenzo wouldn't have gone out looking for him. If Lorenzo hadn't gone out, then the mob would not have found and beaten him to death.

Francisco forces himself to open his eyes, to look at the mangled body again. Lorenzo must have bled out alone on the side of the road. Francisco hopes that, in his friend's final moments, the pain faded and his soul slipped gently away. That his last thoughts were not of this lonely, migratory life—so different from what they'd all imagined when they left the islands—and not of greedy gambling house proprietors or stingy growers or thieving contractors or angry white mobs.

He hopes instead that Lorenzo remembered home. The Pia-aw Falls and the Cabulalaan Hills. The white-sand coastline of Cabangtalan Beach and the cobblestoned streets of Vigan. His lolo's poems and his lola's cooking. And all the other things from back home he used to tell Francisco about in the cool, clear evenings or the foggy early mornings when the world was quiet and the future stretched out ahead of them like the open sea.

And then the questions begin.

"Does he have any family here?"

"Do you know where he would want to be buried?"

"What do you want to do?"

Francisco closes his eyes again. Clenches his jaws. He can't do this. Not now. Not ever.

Thankfully one of the old-timers covers the body again and tells the others to shut up, to give Francisco space to grieve his friend.

Without a word, Francisco wipes his eyes, pushes himself back to his feet. He looks at his friend one more time—then leaves, ignoring the old-timer's invitation to stay as coldly as he ignores the questions about what is to be done with the body.

He limps all the way back to his bunkhouse, alone and broken. He ignores the questions from the others, gathers his few possessions, and walks out the door. Head filled with a red haze, Francisco wanders to the rails, to the bend where the trains slow down.

This is not how it was supposed to be. This is not the America he imagined, the America he was sold. He came here to gain; instead, he's lost so much: land, family, home, earnings, jobs, Milly, Bea, Lorenzo, dignity, hope. All in one year. How many other losses loom on the horizon the longer he stays? After ten or twenty more years in this country, would anything of his—of him—remain?

He should never have left. He was a stupid boy who believed flimsy lies. This country is not an opportunity. It is a trap. A poisoned promise laced with lies.

He wants to hurt, to kill, or—even worse—to force them to feel his pain. And not only those who murdered Lorenzo but all those who lure and prey and exploit and hoard and destroy. Even all those who shrug and do nothing. Even their children. No matter their nationality or race. The colonizers and the contractors, the recruiters and the thieves, the growers and the gangsters, the bankers and the bootleggers, the pimps and the police and the politicians.

Like a seed buried in his heart, his anger grows, takes root, blossoms barbed with thorns.

He won't stall any longer. He'll make his way to San Francisco and do whatever it takes to get back onto a ship that will carry him home. Forget this place.

A whistle pierces the air, pulling Francisco out of himself. He looks up, spots the northbound train on the tracks in the distance. The sound grows louder as it approaches, and soon Francisco can feel the rumbling through his feet. As expected, it slows at the bend, metal grinding against metal. As the engine passes, Francisco begins to run, slow enough to let the clanking boxcars pass until he spots an empty one with open doors.

He matches its speed and readies himself to hop in, to leave this place behind forever.

But when the moment comes to jump, he remembers Lorenzo's words from last night: *If you really want to fight back, little brother, then stay.*

Francisco slows, letting the empty boxcar roll past. A few cars later, there's another one. But he recalls his friend's voice once again: *They want you to leave.*

And, again, Francisco does not jump.

What would going home now accomplish? He'd be a failure on both shores.

The last train car begins to pass. His last chance.

But he can't stop thinking about Lorenzo urging him to stay.

Francisco slows to a jog, then to a walk. The train whooshes past. Its clacking and churning fades as it disappears into the distance. In its quiet wake, the haze that has been fogging Francisco's mind clears.

He will stay.

He will stay, and he will fight the fight his friend no longer can.

Except he will fight it in his own way because Lorenzo wasn't right about everything. The white people who believe this country is theirs alone will never let the Filipinos live their lives in peace. No matter how educated they become, how much money they make, how many businesses they build.

There is no going back.

This is his home now.

It will be whatever he makes of it.

ENZO

May 2020
Philadelphia, PA

GROWN-ASS MEN

At first Enzo thinks he imagined the knocking on the living room window. But then it comes again: four quick raps that rattle the glass in its ancient wooden frame.

He sets his phone down. Still wrapped in his blankets, he goes to the window and pulls back the curtain. Kyle is on the other side, standing on Enzo's porch, a KN95 mask covering most of his face. He waves as his eyes crinkle at the corners with a smile Enzo can't see.

Enzo moves to open the door, but Kyle gestures for him to stop. He holds up his phone instead and shows Enzo that he's calling.

It's been easy enough to ignore texts or online messages, but to ignore his friend when he's standing right in front of him would be a real asshole move. So Enzo grabs his phone and hits accept. "What's up?"

"Hey, man," comes his friend's voice. He sounds relieved, as if he didn't think Enzo would answer. "Didn't want you to open the door because of this global pandemic and all."

"Oh, that's still happening?" Enzo asks dryly.

"Glad to know isolation hasn't dulled your razor-sharp wit."

Enzo shrugs even though they're on the phone, since they can see each other through the window. "Everything okay?"

"You tell me."

Enzo doesn't reply.

"You've dropped off the face of the earth, man," Kyle says.

"So did you."

"Yeah, sorry about that. But I came back. You haven't yet."

Enzo is quiet.

"Anyway," Kyle goes on, "your mom said you were still alive, but I wanted to see for myself."

"You spoke with my mom?"

"That's not all we did."

Enzo closes the curtain.

"Sorry, sorry, sorry," Kyle says. "Low-hanging fruit. Can I please see your beautiful unshowered face again?"

Slowly, Enzo pulls back the curtain. How long *has* it been since he showered?

"Thank you," Kyle says. "But for real, man, how are you?"

Enzo wants to tell Kyle about the disastrous walk with Chris and Lolo Emil and about how he's been spiraling ever since, but he doesn't want to be a burden. Maybe he's too much sometimes.

"I'll be fine," he says, dodging the question.

Kyle sighs. "Murder hornets back?"

Enzo nods. But instead of elaborating, he asks, "And how are you?"

"Not gonna lie, it's been rough. You know I'm an extrovert, so I have all this pent-up energy from not hanging out with people. I've been doing a lot of virtual stuff, but it isn't the same, and all that time on the computer's been giving me a massive headache. I bought these blue-light-blocking glasses, and they've been helping a bit. But still. My soul needs to be with people, you know?"

Enzo nods again. He's definitely more of an introvert, but even this through-the-window hangout with Kyle reminds him how much he's missed being in the physical presence of someone he trusts and cares about. "So does anything help you feel better?" he asks.

Kyle considers the question. "Yoga. Jogging. Smoothies. Petting my cats. Talking on the phone instead of just texting. I've gotten really into baking sourdough."

Enzo remembers a tweet he saw about how self-care can't save the world, can't repair unjust systems, but he doesn't interrupt.

"And," Kyle continues, "neither of my dads are traveling for work anymore, so we've been spending a lot more time together. Family game nights and movie nights and stuff like that. We even started going on walks together, just like you and your grandfather. You were right—it's actually been really good, and we've been learning a lot about each other."

"That's cool," Enzo says. "But my lolo and I aren't doing that anymore."

"For real?"

"For real."

"What happened?"

Enzo tells him about inviting his dad along and how that blew up in his face and made things so much worse, none of them talking to one another at all now.

"Damn," Kyle says when Enzo finishes the story. "Sorry to hear. It must be hard for you to carry all that."

"All of what?" Enzo asks.

"You're, like, trying to fix your family," Kyle says.

"As if that's possible."

"Dude, you're sixteen." Kyle shakes his head. "It's cool that you tried, but it's too much to put on yourself. You can't force these two grown-ass men to change after who knows how long that they've been living like that."

"I'm supposed to just let things suck?" Enzo asks.

"Maybe. For now at least. And if you're going to keep trying, I think you have to accept that it'll definitely take more than one walk."

Enzo considers this. It reminds him of what his therapist is always saying about big fish swimming in deeper waters and about how, when it comes to repairing relationships, you can keep the door open, but you can't make the other person walk through it.

"Thanks, Kyle," Enzo says, feeling a bit lighter. "That makes sense."

Kyle presses his fist to the window, and Enzo bumps his own softly against the other side of the glass.

"Love you, bro."

"Love you, too, bro."

EVERYTHING WE NEVER HAD

It's a little past two in the morning. Enzo is doomscrolling on the couch when he hears a set of footsteps descend the creaky wooden stairs. He expects whoever it is to turn toward either him or the kitchen when they reach the first floor, but instead there's the soft click of the dead bolt, followed by the door quietly swinging open, then closed.

Enzo pockets his phone and eases himself off the couch. He goes to the front window, peeks through the curtains. In the semidarkness of streetlights and shadows, his dad sits on the top of their stoop, barefoot, in basketball shorts and a hoodie, the amber glow of a cigarette at his fingertips.

Guess he's having trouble sleeping these days too.

Enzo lets the curtains fall closed and is about to return to the couch when he hears the low murmur of his dad's voice on the other side of the glass. He must be on the phone, but who would he be talking to at this hour?

Enzo peeks out the window again. Chris isn't pressing his phone to his ear. He's not even holding a phone or wearing earbuds.

Shifting his angle, Enzo sees that his dad isn't alone—someone is sitting in one of the chairs on the other side of the porch: Lolo Emil.

When did the old man go outside? Enzo must have drifted off for a few minutes at some point. He had been on the couch all night and hadn't heard Lolo Emil walk past.

But Lolo Emil and Chris are incapable of speaking to each other one-on-one. Why would his dad *choose* to join the old man out on the porch in the middle of the night?

Enzo listens at the window. Their muffled voices go back and forth. Neither sounds angry, but the conversation is too quiet to hear through the glass. Enzo considers opening it, but the old wooden frame often sticks in the springtime humidity, and he doesn't want them to know he's there.

Instead Enzo slips out the back door barefoot and creeps along the side of the house, grateful that they live at the end of the row. When he reaches the front edge of the sidewall, he sits down silently, out of sight. He crosses his legs, rests his back against the cool brick, and stares at the ground.

"He's a child," Lolo Emil is saying. "I'm not going to apologize to a child."

The familiar tightness pinches Enzo's chest as he realizes they are talking about him. Does he really want to hear what they say when he's not there? He considers going back inside—but decides to stay.

Several seconds of silence pass before Chris responds. "If a person makes a mistake, they should apologize, Dad. How hard is that to understand? Doesn't matter how old either person is."

"And what mistake did I make, Christopher?"

Chris sighs. "He wanted all three of us to spend time together. And we just ended up fighting."

Lolo Emil coughs a few times, then clears his throat. "That wasn't my fault."

"It was both of our faults."

"No. Eric and I had been getting on fine before that night. You were the one who came in with the attitude. And then I only wanted to follow the same route we'd been following twice a day for weeks, but you wanted to switch things up for no reason."

"I had a reason, Dad! The park—" Chris stops himself. Exhales. "I don't want to argue about that walk."

"Then what do you want, Christopher? Why did you come out here?"

"I want you to understand that your grandson is not doing well."

Ah. So his dad has noticed, even if he hasn't said anything directly to Enzo.

Lolo Emil coughs and coughs. "And?"

"And you—*we*—can do something to help him."

"You honestly think the two of us apologizing to that boy for getting into a simple argument is going to fix him?"

Chris lets out a short angry burst of laughter. "God, Dad, how many times do I have to tell you? It's not about fixing him. It's about doing what's right."

"It's not my fault he's so . . . sensitive."

"You say that like it's a bad thing."

"Isn't it?"

"No—it's beautiful."

Enzo looks up. There's the moon. Nearly full, ripe with light, peeking between tree branches and power lines. Tears well in his eyes. If his dad really thinks this, then why hasn't he ever said it to him?

"Beautiful?" Lolo Emil scoffs. "It's weakness, Christopher. Your coddling isn't preparing him for real life. Softness doesn't survive this world."

"It's not coddling—it's letting him be who he is rather than trying to force him to be someone he isn't."

"Ah, I see. This again. What you always like to think your mother and I did to you."

"It's what *you* tried to do. Mom just let it happen."

"We tried to give you and your sisters everything we never had. You're here because of us. You should see what happened to my cousins who never went to college, who never left the Central Valley. Did I ever tell you about Leon? Not long after he came back from Vietnam, he overdosed and left behind four kids. *Four.* Let that sink in. Is that the father you would have wanted? Is that the life you would have wanted?"

Chris takes a long drag. "I don't even know Leon's story, Dad, so I'm not about to judge him. But I don't disagree with you about trying to give my child everything I never had. I do think that's our job as parents, from one generation to the next. But to me, it's not only about the material."

"Oh? Then what's it about?"

"Love."

Lolo Emil lets out a sarcastic laugh. "I made sure you grew up in a safe neighborhood with good schools. That you could focus on your studies instead of needing a job. That you always had a fridge full of food. That you could go to the doctor when you were sick. That you didn't have to worry about paying for college—even if I thought your major was useless."

"And I appreciate all that, Dad."

"But that wasn't enough for you? That wasn't . . . 'love'?" Enzo imagines Lolo Emil wincing as he says the last word. In his entire life, had he ever said it to anyone besides Grandma Linda and maybe his own mom? If not, how sad.

"In some ways, sure," Chris says. "But there's more to it."

"Enlighten me."

"So, yeah, it's doing all that stuff you did to take care of someone. But it's also knowing them. Like, really, truly understanding them as a person as much as possible. It's getting out of the way and allowing them the freedom to be that person. It's being proud, not when they fulfill your own expectations or conditions but when they live in a way that aligns with who they are. It's a whole lot of other stuff, too, that I can't put into words. That's the love I'm trying to give to Enzo, at least."

Lolo Emil speaks again, this time with uncharacteristic concern. "I never gave you any of that, Christopher?"

"No, Dad," Chris says without missing a beat. "You didn't."

It's quiet for a long time. Then Lolo Emil asks in a voice with as much resentment as regret, "Is that why we'll never have what you and Enzo have?"

Chris sighs. "I think so."

Another silence arrives, heavy with history.

Lolo Emil clears his throat. "Soon as I can arrange everything," he says, his tone hardened, "I'm moving back into the retirement home."

"Wait—what?" Chris asks. "Where did that come from?"

"It's clear I'm not wanted here."

"Dad, that's not what—and the pandemic is still—"

A chair scrapes, footsteps sound, the front door opens—and slams shut.

Chris scoffs. Snuffs out his cigarette. Takes out another one. There's the flick of a lighter, then cigarette paper burning with the first inhale. He blows out the smoke in a long, slow exhale, and it drifts out over Enzo's head, veiling his view of the moon.

Enzo wants to go to his dad. To thank him for everything he said even if he didn't say it to Enzo, for defending him, for everything Chris has been trying to do. It's been imperfect, but what isn't?

Maybe Lolo Emil is right about sensitivity as weakness. Maybe not. Enzo only knows that in this moment his heart swells. He pushes off the wall and onto his feet, startling Chris.

"Enzo?" Chris asks. "What are you doing out here?"

Enzo walks up the steps and sits next to Chris. He leans his head against his dad's shoulders, feels them relax.

Chris puts an arm around Enzo and kisses his son's head like he used to do when Enzo was little. "How much of that did you hear?" Chris asks.

"Most of it."

"I wasn't trying to make him leave."

Enzo sighs. "We can try to talk to him in the morning."

"Sure. But you know how he is—I don't think we'll have much success trying to change his mind."

"I know. But we can try."

Chris is quiet for a few moments. He sniffs. Rubs his eyes. Pulls up his hood. "Have I ever told you about Calauit Island?"

"I don't think so."

"It's in Palawan. Back in the seventies, Marcos kicked out hundreds of Indigenous people whose ancestors had lived there since time immemorial. Then he illegally bought a bunch of African animals—giraffes, zebras, gazelles, and so on—and shipped them to Calauit. It became the Marcos family's own private safari park."

"That's messed up."

"Sure was. And after the People Power Revolution ousted Marcos in

'86, it didn't get much better. It became a public tourist attraction, but there wasn't enough funding to ensure the animals were well taken care of. Plus the Tagbanua—the people indigenous to the island—kept trying to reclaim the land by sabotaging the park and hunting the animals. The Philippine government didn't like that and would kill the Tagbanua in retribution. All that's *still* going on today."

Enzo doesn't know what to say. It's depressing as hell, the way terrible decisions from the past can ripple through time, fucking everything up forever.

"Anyway," Chris says, "that's what my relationship with your lolo feels like sometimes."

Enzo considers this interpretation. It makes sense, but does that make him the animals in this metaphor?

"I don't want us to be that, Enzo."

"We're not, Dad."

"Ever."

"We won't be."

Chris takes one final drag from his cigarette, then snuffs it out in the mug. He pulls down his hood. "I love you. I'm sorry I don't say that enough. I'm sorry that I'm not very good at opening up on a deeper level. But know that I'm trying, and that I'll try harder."

"I know, Dad, and I think I understand better now why that is. But I love you too."

Chris hugs Enzo closer. "I really do think it's beautiful that you're so sensitive, that you can feel things so deeply. I admire it. Never let anyone make you think it's a weakness. If anything, it's a superpower. The world would be a much better place if there were more men like you than like me or your lolo."

The moon shifts. The smoke clears. They stay on the porch for some time, Chris's arm staying around Enzo, Enzo's head staying on Chris's shoulder. Silence returns, but this time it's a silence with a shore on the other side.

WHOLE

The next day, Enzo's dad texts him a link. Chris often does this. Sometimes they're articles, sometimes memes from Facebook Enzo already saw weeks ago on TikTok. Enzo usually ignores them, wondering if his dad's familiar with the law of diminishing returns. But this time the preview image catches his attention. It shows a family of boars casually strolling through an empty downtown street.

Turns out it's an article about the impact of the community-wide quarantines on nature. It opens with a standalone quote from someone named Aldo Leopold: "We abuse land because we regard it as a commodity belonging to us. When we see land as a community to which we belong, we may begin to use it with love and respect."

The author opens by talking about a few Photoshopped images of wild animals in urban areas that have recently gone viral, claiming that nature was making a comeback thanks to the massive decrease in human activity all around the world. But then they begin talking about all the ways this is untrue. Animals scrambling to survive after having become over-dependent on eating scraps of human food. Conservation programs put on pause. The expected increase in poaching and deforestation and illegal mining, particularly in the Global South. And other massively depressing consequences.

Why would his dad send him this when he's obviously been struggling with his mental health? Maybe Chris just saw the cute animal photos and didn't actually read the piece? Wouldn't be the first time.

But Enzo keeps going, and the tone shifts. It describes increased bee populations. Lower carbon emissions. Ocean animals enjoying calmer waters, ranging farther than usual. Bears, deer, and bison reclaiming closed national parks in the US. Bats returning to caves they'd been absent from for decades. And more.

The author concludes by cautioning their readers not to get too caught up with the feel-good viral posts declaring that nature has been restored but also not to wallow in the despair of the very real negative consequences. Both sets of facts are simultaneously true. Both feelings can be felt alongside each other. Instead the writer encourages the world to view this pause as a reset, a chance to collectively reflect and reevaluate our relationship with the natural world.

At the end of the article is another standalone quote from Aldo Leopold: "We shall never achieve harmony with the land, any more than we shall achieve absolute justice or liberty for people. In these higher aspirations, the important thing is not to achieve but to strive."

Enzo makes a note to read more Aldo Leopold, then texts his dad.
Interesting.

Chris replies, **Love you, anak.**

Love you, too, Dad.

Three days later they finalize the arrangements with the retirement home, and Lolo Emil's luggage is loaded back into the car. It's a chilly morning. Vapor rises from the damp streets and sidewalks as the overnight rain evaporates in the sunlight. Chris waits behind the wheel as the old man and his dog say their goodbyes to Julia and Enzo.

"You sure you don't want to stay, Lolo?" Enzo tries one last time.

"I've already overstayed my welcome," Lolo Emil says, walls firmly back in place. "Time for me to go."

Thor whines and nuzzles against Enzo's legs. Enzo scratches him behind the ears. "I'll miss our walks."

Lolo Emil nods and hugs Enzo. When they pull apart, Lolo Emil holds out the leash.

Enzo looks at it, confused.

"I want you to take care of him," Lolo Emil explains.

"Wait, you mean—"

Lolo Emil swallows. Nods.

"I can't ta—"

"I want you to, Enzo."

Julia and Chris start to protest, but Lolo Emil cuts them off. "You need each other."

Enzo's parents exchange a look. They know he's right.

"Are you sure, Dad?" Chris asks.

"I am."

Julia gestures at Enzo to go ahead, and Enzo takes the leash. "Thank you."

Lolo Emil kisses Thor on the top of the nose one more time and whispers, "Ingat." Then he climbs into the car. "But make sure to bring him by to visit me," he tells Enzo before turning away.

"For sure," Enzo says.

And then they're gone.

No more pill bottles. No more slippers shuffling across the floor. No more hacking cough or reality shows about hoarders blaring too loudly. No more walks with the old man.

Enzo's room is entirely his own again. He moves everything back into its place. The chair by the window. The bookshelf. The bamboo palm. His journal. Next to the chair, he sets up a dog bed for Thor using an old comforter. Then he sits down and googles how to downgrade to an old-school flip phone.

A collective sadness settles over the household. Enzo and his parents eat dinner quietly. They clear the table slowly. They wash the dishes mournfully. Then Enzo takes Thor for his evening walk alone.

As frustrating as the old man's presence was, nobody wanted him gone—they wanted him whole.

CLEAR

One night, as soon as the last dish is dried and put away, Chris grabs his pack of cigarettes and lighter. But before he reaches the back door, Enzo calls to him, "Walk with us?"

Chris pauses. Sets down the cigarettes and lighter. "Of course."

Enzo smiles, clips on Thor's leash, then turns to Julia. "Mom?"

But she's already settling onto the couch with a book. "Another time. You guys go ahead."

It's still light out, and there's a touch of wildness about the city. Uncut grass. Untrimmed trees. Quiet streets. Thor sniffs everything, pleased by every inch of the world.

Enzo hopes his and his dad's desires to be better for each other will last, just as he hopes Lolo Emil and Chris will eventually try to work on their relationship. He doesn't know for sure if either will happen. These days he doesn't even know what's going to happen next week. But he's learning to be okay with that and with the idea that some things get worse before they can get better.

And he's learning to go easy on his grandfather, on his father, on himself. His conversations with his lolo and that late-night talk with his dad have helped him understand how the present is the past is the future.

As he and his dad walk on together, sharing a comfortable silence, Enzo notices for the first time in months that his chest feels relaxed; his mind, quiet and clear. It's a fragile peace, one he'll take when he can.

Eventually they reach the intersection where Chris and Lolo Emil had argued about where to go. But instead of leading them down the street toward the park or taking the route Enzo used to follow with Lolo Emil, Chris turns to Enzo.

"Which way?"

AUTHOR'S NOTE

Though the Maghabols are an imagined family, the historical settings through which they move are based in fact. I tried to understand and portray these events as accurately as I could, but the story you hold in your hands is ultimately a work of fiction. I've included a list of recommended texts and resources through which you can learn much more about the Manong Generation, the Watsonville riots, Stockton's Little Manila, the Delano grape strike, the Ferdinand Marcos dictatorship, the assassination of Benigno Aquino, Jr., and the rise in anti-Asian hate crimes during the COVID-19 pandemic.

Lorenzo Tolentino is also fictional, but the violence he and the others experienced was real. His character was inspired by Fermin Tobera, whose death was the only documented murder that occurred during the Watsonville riots. Little is known about Tobera beyond that he was born in Ilocos Sur in 1908, immigrated to the United States in 1928, worked in the fields, and was shot through the heart by a group of white men who attacked his bunkhouse on January 23, 1930. His body was returned to the Philippines at the request of his mother, Valentina Ibarra, spurring protests demanding justice for Tobera and other Filipinos laboring under oppressive and racist conditions in the United States. I hope this story helps honor Fermin Tobera's memory and the lives of the other manongs.

While the manongs helped establish a place for Filipinos in the United

States, we must remember that we have a long history on the continent that predates the twentieth century. On October 18, 1587, the first Filipinos stepped foot in North America, according to recorded history (which is why October is Filipino American History Month). They were sailors—some of whom may have been enslaved—on a Spanish galleon that docked in what is now Morro Bay, California. The crew retreated to their ships within two days, after conflicts with a group of the Indigenous Chumash people, who had inhabited the region for over ten thousand years. Throughout the 1700s, Filipinos escaping from such Spanish ships established a presence in Louisiana, eventually forming a community of their own called St. Malo, outside of what is now New Orleans. A Filipino named Antonio Miranda Rodriguez was among those sent by the Spanish government in 1781 to establish what is now Los Angeles. All that to say, *Everything We Never Had* begins almost one hundred years ago, but our story in this country spans over four centuries.

Mga Utang Ng Loob

Thank you to the ancestors, both the personal and the collective. I believe all Filipino Americans—and all Americans—should remember and honor the Filipinos who fought to be more than a source of cheap labor. Filipino American history is American history.

To my agent, Beth Phelan, thank you for your support, advice, and advocacy. I'm a better writer and publishing is a better industry because of you. To my editor, Namrata Tripathi, thank you for seeing the potential in the seed of an idea, and thank you for your invaluable feedback and questions along the way. This story wouldn't be the same without you—in fact, it might not even exist. Thank you as well to the rest of Team Kokila: Asiya Ahmed, Tenisha Anderson-Kenkpen, Joanna Cárdenas, Zareen Jaffery, Jenny Ly, Sydnee Monday, and Jasmin Rubero. Thank you, Theresa Evangelista, for the beautiful cover design, and thank you, Julian Callos, for the stunning cover art. Thank you to Ariela Rudy Zaltzman and Kaitlyn San Miguel for chasing down my grammatical issues and inconsistencies. Thank you to my publicist, Kaitlin Kneafsey, and the entire Penguin School & Library Marketing team—Venessa Carson, Andrea Cruise, Judith Huerta, Carmela Iaria, Trevor Ingerson, Summer Ogata, Gaby Paez, and Danielle Presley—for connecting teachers, librarians, and students with my words.

Thank you to the writers and their works which greatly influenced the vision I had for this novel from the outset: Jean Toomer's *Cane*, Sandra Cisneros's *The House on Mango Street*, and Jacqueline Woodson's *Red at the Bone*. Thank you to those at the Tobera Project and Watsonville is in the Heart digital archives—especially Roy Recio and Meleia Simon-Reynolds—for teaching me about Watsonville, answering my questions, and giving me feedback. Your archives and events are absolute treasures, and your work serves as a model for what university-community partnerships can be. And thank you, Roy, for the intergenerational fishing idea. Thank you to Olivia Sawi for your presentation on the Watsonville riots. Thank you to Dillon Delvo for showing me around Stockton and Little Manila, and thank you to FANHS-Silicon Valley and Manong Robert for the Pinoytown walking tour. To my research assistant, Skya Theobald, thank you for all the hours you spent filling in my (many) gaps of knowledge as I drafted. Thank you to Teresito Custodia, Diosdado M. Domingo, Maria Teresa N. Domingo, Luisa A. Igloria, and others for helping with the Ilokano. To Roberto Ribay and Rosa Seyfried, thank you for the help with the Tagalog and the Spanish, respectively. Thank you to Traci Chee for providing valuable feedback on a later draft to help me refine the plot. To Dr. Ariel Baptiste, thank you for providing feedback on the novel's depiction of mental health, and to Dr. Jean-Arellia Tolentino and Kate Viernes, thank you for helping me with my own mental health in ways that became intertwined with this story. As always, all mistakes are my own.

Thank you to Stacey Lee for sharing your insights on historical fiction. Thank you to Barbara Jane Reyes for your Pinay lit course, which helped me think more deeply about the women in my novel even as I wrote a book focused on father-son relationships. Thank you to Neal Shusterman, Ebony Elizabeth Thomas, Joan Trygg, and Colleen AF Venable for our (somewhat) monthly virtual book club/check-in meetings. Thank you to Joanna Ho, Parker Peevyhouse, and Caroline Pritchard for our in-person writing sessions, and thank you to the entire Bay Area Kid Lit crew for the community. Thank you to all the readers, students, educators, reviewers, and booksellers who've shown love to my books over the years.

To my family and friends and former students, thank you for continuing to support and champion my writing across continents. To my wife, Kathryn, thank you for your ongoing insight, encouragement, and love. You keep me going when things on the page and in life fail to make sense.

To my father, Roberto Ribay, thank you for encouraging my interests, showing up to all the games and matches and tournaments, cooking Filipino food and taking us to the Philippines, teaching me the importance of hard work and discipline, and for everything else you did and continue to do.

Finally, to my son, Felix, thank you for coming into my life. Every day you make me think deeply about the kind of father and human I want to be, a process which was the driving force behind this narrative. I've made—and will continue to make—countless mistakes, but know that I love you so much, no matter what.

Recommended Resources

Texts:

The Delano Manongs (2014) directed by Marissa Aroy for PBS

America Is in the Heart by Carlos Bulosan

Dollar a Day, 10 Cents a Dance (1984) directed by Geoffrey Dunn and Mark Schwartz

"Empire and the Moving Body: Fermin Tobera, Military California, and Rural Space" by Dorothy B. Fujita-Rony from *Making the Empire Work: Labor and United States Imperialism*, edited by Daniel E. Bender and Jana K. Lipman

The Pain We Carry: Healing from Complex PTSD for People of Color by Natalie Y. Gutiérrez

The Will to Change: Men, Masculinity, and Love by bell hooks

Little Manila Is in the Heart: The Making of the Filipina/o Community in Stockton, California by Dawn Bohulano Mabalon

Journey for Justice: The Life of Larry Itliong by Dawn Bohulano Mabalon and Gayle Romasanta, illustrated by Andre Sibayan

The Conjugal Dictatorship of Ferdinand and Imelda Marcos by Primitivo Mijares

Tomorrow's Memories: A Diary, 1924–1928 by Angeles Monrayo

Online Resources:

Asian Mental Health Collective at https://asianmhc.org

Filipino American National Historical Society at http://www.fanhs-national.org/history.html

Little Manila Rising at https://littlemanila.org

Migrante USA at https://migranteusa.org

Pilipino Association of Workers and Immigrants at https://pawis-sv.com

Stop AAPI Hate at https://stopaapihate.org

Therapin*y at https://therapinay.com

The Tobera Project at https://www.toberaproject.com

United Farm Workers at https://ufw.org

Watsonville is in the Heart digital archives at https://wiith.ucsc.edu

Broadcast from the chapter "I May Not Be Able to Talk to You Again After This" excerpted from *NBC Evening News*, August 21, 1983, accessed through the Vanderbilt Television News Archive.